FICTION HOUSE PRESS
PRESENTS

SPICY STORIES

September 1934
Vol. IV, No. 9

This reprint edition is a facsimile of the original pulp magazine. Variations in printing and quality can be attributed to the original magazine which was printed on rough woodpulp paper.

ISBN 978-1-64720-106-7

www.FictionHousePress.com
fictionhousepress@gmail.com

"Stop Worrying . . .

NOW I CAN TELL YOU THE TRUE FACTS ABOUT

SEX!

WOULD YOU like to know the *whole truth* about sex? All of the startling facts that even the frankest books have heretofore not dared to print are explained in clear, scientific manner, vividly illustrated, in the revolutionary book — "The New Eugenics". Here at last, the naked truth stands forth, stripped of all prudery and narrow prejudice. Old fashioned taboos are discarded and the subject of sex is brought out into the bright light of medical science by Dr. C. S. Whitehead M.D. and Dr. Charles A. Hoff, M.D., the authors!

SEX ATTRACTION!

Sex appeal and sex satisfaction are the *most powerful forces* in your life. To remain in ignorance is to remain in danger of lifelong suffering. It is the purpose of this great book to show sex-ignorant men and women how to enjoy safely the thrilling experiences that are their birthright. It not only tells you how to *attract the opposite sex*, but also how to *hold the love of your mate* throughout a *blissful married life*.

DANGEROUS!

. . . Unless you know the true facts about sex! Ignorance leads to shame, despair, worry and remorse.

Do you know how to add variety to your love-making? The most innocent kiss may lead to tragedy if you are ignorant of sex relations.

Will FEAR

grip you on your wedding night? . . . or will it be the tender, thrilling experience that is your birthright!

Banish Fear and Sex Ignorance Forever!

SEX IS NO LONGER a mysterious sin, mentioned only in the conversational gutters — it is the most powerful force in the world and can be made the most beautiful. Thanks to this bravely written book, it is no longer necessary to pay the awful price for one moment of bliss. Science now lights the path to knowledge and lifelong sex happiness.

LOVE MAKING IS AN ART!

Are you an *awkard novice* in the art of love making or a master of its difficult technique? The art of love-making takes *skill* and *knowledge*. The sexual embrace as practiced by those ignorant of its true scientific importance is crude, awkward and *often terrifying* to more sensitive natures. Normal sex-suited people are torn apart because they lack the knowledge that makes for a happy sex life!

Sex Facts for Men and Women

Twilight Sleep—Easy Childbirth
Sex Excesses
The Crime of Abortion
Impotence and Sex Weakness
Secrets of the Honeymoon
Teaching Children Sex
The Dangers of Petting
What Every Man Should Know
The Truth about Masturbation
Venereal Diseases
The Sexual Embrace
How to Build Virility
How to Gain Greater Delight
What to Allow a Lover To Do
Birth Control Chart for Married Women

SEND NO MONEY!

You send no money — just fill out the coupon below and then when it arrives, in plain wrapper, pay the postman $1.98. Keep the book five days, then if you are not satisfied send it back and we will refund your money immediately and without question. This book NOT sold to minors.

640 DARING PAGES!

98 VIVID PICTURES!

PIONEER PUBLISHING COMPANY
Dept. PS-9 1270 Sixth Ave., New York, N.Y.

Send me the "The New Eugenics" in plain wrapper. I will pay postman $1.98 (plus postage) on delivery. If I am not completely satisfied, I can return the book within five days and the entire price will be refunded immediately. Also send me, FREE of CHARGE, your book "The Philosophy of Life".

Name ______________________

Address ______________ *Age*

Foreign Orders 10 shillings in advance.

FREE! **PHILOSOPHY OF LIFE**

This astonishing book, telling frankly and clearly the difference in construction and function of man and woman, is sent without cost to all who order "The New Eugenics" at $1.98. All about the thrilling mystery of Sex! FREE!

PIONEER PUBLISHING CO.
Radio City
1270 Sixth Avenue, New York

SEPTEMBER
1934
VOLUME IV
NUMBER 9

PEPPY STORIES

A SPARKLING FEATURE

SPICY STORIES is published monthly by the D. M. Publishing Co., Inc., Wilmington, Del. William J. David, President.

Between You and Me!

Dear Editor:

Today I purchased my first copy of Spicy Stories and am more than delighted to say the least with its many thrilling stories. I am also interested in the "Between You and Me" page contained in Spicy Stories, and would ask that you please print this letter in your next issue, as I would like very much to correspond with widows, maidens and any others of the female sex who would care to cheer up a very lonely bachelor.

I am 43 years of age, blond with blue eyes, 5 ft. 9 in. in height, and weigh 194 lbs., and would be only too happy to answer all letters received immediately. I am very broadminded, so those who write to me can make their letters as interesting as they care to, and then see what they receive in return, as I have had plenty of experiences and thrills in my days. So get busy you widows, maidens and girlies, and let me hear from you very soon, will you please?

Hoping to be showered with plenty of letters from the opposite sex, and wishing your Spicy Stories all the success it duly deserves, I remain,

Yours truly,

Frank Dunn.

10405 *Joan Ave., Cleveland, Ohio.*

Dear Editor:

I am a constant reader of Spicy, Pep, etc., and enjoy them very much. May they never stop.

As I am lonesome I would like to receive letters from girls, ages unlimited. I am old enough to have a little fun and I'm not hard to look at. I have light hair, grey eyes, am 5 ft. 8 in. tall, and weigh 140 pounds.

So come on, girls, and write me some snappy letters. Will exchange snapshots.

A reader,

Leo Guthrie.

Esbon, Kansas.

P. S.—A prize for the girl who sends the snappiest letter.

Dear Sir:

As an ardent reader of "Spicy" magazine, I wish to congratulate you on the turnout of a very interesting book. The stories, besides being "spicy," are put in such a way that they make good reading, which I am sure will make your magazine more popular than ever.

I can assure you that when the book seller comes around the boys simply dive for "Spicy", and it helps them to forget the thousands of miles which separate them from home.

If some of the fairer sex would like a pen pal, I am at their service, and I could relate to them some weird and wonderful experiences. Of course I would like a photo, and if Patricia, P. O. Box 3, Dumont, N. J., cares to write, I would be very much obliged. Wishing you all the best in the near future,

I am, yours sincerely,

Walter Finch.

D(MG) Company, Napier Barracks, Lahore Cantts, India.

Dear Sisters of the Modern Age:

I get so much thrill out of Spicy magazine. It is so wonderful that I can hardly wait until it is on the newsstand every month.

I also read Pep, Snappy, La Paree and Gay Parisienne. They are also just what the people have been looking for.

I am a young lady 22 years of age, weigh 122 pounds, 5 ft. 6 in. tall, a wonderful figure, dark red curly hair and brown eyes.

I have had lots of thrilling experiences with both girls and boys. Have traveled a lot. I would like to hear from other people who have been places.

Miss Mary Hale.

P. O. Box 242, Mt. Pleasant, Mich.

Dear Editor:

As a regular reader of "Spicy" allow me to say that it is one of the goldingdest humdingers of all the magazines. I enjoy it from cover to cover.

I'd like very much to hear from any of the fair readers anywhere—especially those who live in Massachusetts. But no matter where you are, come on girls.

I'm twenty-five years of age, medium tall, brown hair, hazel eyes, and get by all right with my looks. I've had plenty of adventures, so drop me a line and I'll tell you all about them. I'll draw for you too—cartoons, etc.

So just grab your pens and send along

(Please turn to page 62)

SATISFACTORY SUMMER

All night long she lay awake, thinking.

BY GORDON SAYRE

"HOLLYWOOD or no Hollywood; wise girl or no wise girl," Martha White told her cousin, "there's one man at Morency this year that you'd better lay off."

Sandra looked interested: "What's his name? I'll hunt him up immediately."

"His name is Hyde Swan, and you won't have to hunt him up; he can smell a new woman the minute she gets into town. He's liable to pop in any minute. And I'm not kidding about laying off him. He's poison. They say he killed his wife. . . . Oh, I don't mean murdered her . . . he married the prettiest girl in town five years ago. She just sort of shriveled up after their marriage. The last time I saw her alive she weighed about ninety pounds; and she weighed a hundred and a quarter when they were married."

"What is he, a vampire or something?"

"Goodness only knows; he does something to every woman with whom he gets into contact, and one of the things is to just naturally worry her to death. He's a cad. To him a woman is just an object for—"

"How interesting." Sandra observed. She was sitting before her dressing table clad only in brassiere and panties. Her cousin watched her enviously.

"Ye gods," she approved, "Hollywod did you good."

"I'll say it did me good," Sandra confirmed with a cynical little laugh. "Believe me you pay for what you get out that way."

"Well, anyway you got to be a star," Martha pointed out enviously. A dark shadow crossed Sandra's face.

"Yes, I got to be a star."

". . . And you're going to star again when you go back after the summer's over?"

"Yes!" Sandra said it with firmness and decision. "I *am*."

"But," Martha said, "I'll worry about you all the time you're here—this Hyde Swan is the very devil, and you won't take it seriously or believe me. Please let him alone."

"In all probability," Sandra said carelessly, "he'll let me alone."

"No, he won't. He's a born chaser. . . . Been all over the world; knows all the deviltry in that line that there is to be learned on the face of this earth. And when he sees you! . . . God! If he could see you *now!* That way! They certainly know how to build bodies out there in Hollywood. Do you mind taking off that brassiere and those panties for a minute?"

Obligingly Sandra slipped out of her

panties, unfastened her brassiere. Martha gasped.

"You're more beautiful than any statue, any painting of a woman in the nude I ever saw."

Martha walked all around her in admiration; touching the soft, warm, firm flesh here and there. Nowhere was there a blemish to mar the perfection of snowy white skin. From her golden hair to her toenails, perfect and polished like jewels, Sandra was exquisite.

"You ought to be so happy," Martha said, "beautiful, talented, nothing to worry about; a marvelous career attained and lying ahead of you."

"Nothing to worry about is right," Sandra echoed, a trifle cynically. Then she shrugged and went back to her dressing.

"I've been plenty hurt by women in the past; now I strike first."

SURE ENOUGH HYDE SWAN dropped in after dinner. The minute Sandra saw him he did something to her. He was, in point of fact, the devil type; there was certainly no doubt about that. And she liked him instantly; she hadn't expected to find anything so exciting so far away from Hollywood, Miami or New York.

Hyde Swan was tall and slim; there was something pleasantly sharp and angular about him. Sandra, who had needed, since her last contract, to live a circumspect life, in view of the exacting "morality" clause in it, felt something in her bound at sight of him. It did not for a moment occur to her that there was any real danger. Though she had never been promiscuous in a manner indicative of bad taste, she knew a bit about men, and where they are to be found at their worst in Hollywod.

His ears seemed to come to little peaks; and his eyebrows were somewhat sharply arched. His mouth was a thin, firm, cruel straight line. His eyes were gray and cold as steel, though he had a way of heating them for a moment as steel is heated in order to be made malleable—to a white heat. His hair was dark, and he combed it back straightly and sleekly.

He was somewhat pale, and his features were perfectly chiseled. He dressed with that careless faultlessness that spoke of the Continent; and his manners were also quite near perfection.

At once Hyde went into action; in fact, from the moment he acknowledged an introduction; he bent smartly from the waist, and for a moment held her fingers in a firm grasp that was almost painful to her and which yet was not too firm to be in bad taste. A moment later Sandra met her cousin's eyes across the room, and they frantically signaled a warning.

There were many guests, and gradually the after dinner conversation degenerated into small talk. Sandra became bored. Hyde took no part in the conversation. In fact, to her surprise, he rose very early and said lightly:

"Got to be running along . . . going riding tomorrow morning at sun-up; one of my major vices. Love to get up at dawn for a ride through the hills back of town, then come back and sleep till mid afternoon. Do you ride?" he added carelessly, looking at Sandra, as though he were making the remark just out of politeness.

"Love it," Sandra said.

In just the same careless tone he said softly: "Right! I'll call for you at five tomorrow." And then he was gone before she'd even had a chance to say whether or not she would accept.

As soon as he had left Sandra pleaded weariness and went to bed. Martha followed her upstairs.

"Now!" she declaimed, "you've gone and done it!"

"Done what?"

"Gotten yourself in for it."

"I intended to," Sandra said. "You don't for a moment suppose, do you, that Mr. Swan may have met *his* Waterloo, or his Borgia or something."

"But are you really carrying on an affair with Gracie Montrose?"

"Not that man. He wrecks them no matter how sophisticated they are."

Sandra was slipping out of her clothes. In the softly furnished feminine bedroom there was only a shaded lamp lighted for illumination. It suffused the room with a rose glow, wherein Sandra's body seemed a miracle of fleshly patterns. The roundness of her perfect body was revealed in every curve from shoulder to ankle.

When Martha was gone, Sandra surveyed herself thoughtfully. She *was,* she discovered, a bit frightened at this Hyde person . . . but he might serve her purposes admirably—she'd never thought of this way out before coming; but it might be the easiest way after all.

Before donning her pajamas she let her smooth, small hands run caressingly over her velvety hot skin; imagined they were the cruel, firm hands of Hyde Swan, with his long, graceful fingers. She pinched herself experimentally so that it would hurt. Yes, he was the sort who would be cruel in his love-making, and she was inclined to think that she might like it, even though she were made to suffer by it.

When the maid woke Sandra while it was still dark and chilly she got up feeling wretched. It had been years since she'd risen at such an early hour. She wondered if the tendency toward cruelty in Hyde Swan's nature had prompted him to cause her to be waked early so that he could imaginatively enjoy her discomfiture.

Putting on a bathing cap she went into the shower and was about to mix hot and cold water when, whimsically, she decided to make a good job of it and suffer plenty. She turned on the cold water. It was like being pricked with the points of a million sharp icicles. The water sent a fever raging through her blood, however, and she felt better. She donned riding clothes almost gleefully and went downstairs to drink some black coffee.

On the dot Hyde Swan arrived, riding one perfect sleek black horse, and leading a roan. Sandra went out to meet him and for a moment their eyes met in a challenge.

"Didn't think you'd be ready," he complimented, giving her a swiftly appraising look out of his sharp eyes.

"I've never missed location by a minute yet," she smiled. "You'd better lead the way, I know nothing about the roads any more; I've forgotten."

"I'll show you some new roads," Hyde said, and she thought that she caught an overtone of threat in his voice.

When they started out he did not ride beside her. He led the way at a swift canter; the roan had evidently been taught to follow. Sandra let the bridle hang loose, since the horse took every turn without direction, and increased or slackened its speed to agree with that of the lead horse.

Faster and faster their pace grew. Hyde kept always so far ahead that it was impossible for her to call out to him. She began to get angry; she was out of riding practice, and her body began to protest at the unusual strain. But he led the way on and on; over hill and down dale; past wide glimpses of the ocean sparkling in the early morning sunlight. It was all of an hour before he stopped at last at the peak of a hill which looked out over the ocean. The roan trotted up beside the black gelding and came to a stop.

"Well, for goodness' sake!" Sandra protested, "you might have inquired whether I was getting along all right or not."

"Oh, I'm so sorry," he said softly, "but you see I wanted to get you up here for sunrise. It will be any minute now."

He helped her down off the horse and she sat down upon the soft grass, glad to be upon firm earth after the wild ride.

"You *do* look tuckered out," he sympathized. "Why not recline at full length and completely relax for a time?"

Sandra did. He sat down beside her. He looked down at her appreciatively, as though he were about to say: "God! You're beautiful!"

But he said nothing. He just let his eyes glow smolderingly. There was something almost hypnotic about them. Sandra, after her early rising, her cold shower and her wild ride, felt peculiar. The blood tingled and danced through her veins. She began to try to calculate how long it had been since she'd had a *real* adventure, since the signing of her contract with the morality clause, and other annoying clauses in it.

"I've an odd impulse," he told her, just as the sun began to mount resplendently over the ocean horizon. " . . . Know how your hand itches to run over the splendid lines of a beautiful horse?"

"That's a rather doubtful compliment," Sandra observed, suddenly feeling herself athrill at the crudeness of which this man was capable. And then without waiting any further, he half reclined beside her on the turf and one of his hands calmly ran over the swell of her bosom outside the man's shirt she had worn for riding. When she did not protest he permitted himself the pleasure of caressing her litheness throughout.

"If I weren't so tired I'd hit you with my crop," Sandra told him.

"No, you wouldn't," he denied, "because you love it."

"You're taking a lot for granted, aren't you?"

"Very little, as a matter of fact," he assured her, with impudence.

AND THEN SUDDENLY he was at her with a swiftness which caused her instinctively to spring into action. But he was strong and practised. His arms went around her, pinioning her arms to her sides His mouth was over hers And it was only a matter of moments before the intoxication of his kiss had her under its spell. His arms were like steel bands; tighter and tighter they drew until they almost hurt.

"You're taking a lot for granted, aren't you?" she asked.

"Stop it!" she commanded. "Do you think I'm a cheap wench to be taken up here and pawed over this way?"

"I wouldn't have looked at you a second time if I'd sensed anything cheap in you," he told her. "You are an artist; and I, in my own fashion, am an artist too; we're above trifling considerations. Especially alone up here on top of the world, with the clean sun on us, the wide sea before us, and no other human being within eyeshot for miles. Why pretend? I need you. You need me. Can't we abandon the usual banter?"

"You don't seem to intend to give me very much to say about it one way or another."

"No," he agreed, "I don't. If you gave in of your own free will on such short notice you'd feel cheap—whereas if you don't give in and I force you . . . "

And suddenly once more he became active. His warm hand was a creeping patch of live heat over her soft body. His strong fingers clutched her resilient flesh and held it. . . . And his fingers were so talented and quick that presently Sandra felt herself sinking and drowning in a delightful sea of sensation perfumed by the clean fresh smell of the soft grass; lighted by the bright morning light of the sun, given intensity by the fragrant tang of the sea air. The earth beneath them was soft and springy, and Sandra seemed to feel her body taking up strength from the earth.

She struggled no more as his mouth darted everywhere, snuggling into crevices, smoothing bulges; setting her on fire. . . .

"FOR GOODNESS' SAKE! What happened?" Martha asked when Sandra got home in time for luncheon. "Did you fall off your horse or something?"

"No, I'm perfectly all right," Sandra said somewhat listlessly.

"Well you *look* as though you'd had a terrible accident of some kind."

"Did that beast get gay with you?" Martha's husband asked angrily. "If he did I'll—I don't think you ought to go near him, but you're your own master, if you must see him at least he's got to treat *you* decently or he'll answer to me."

Sandra smiled a little tired enigmatical smile.

"I can handle him," she asserted, "and just possibly I'll teach Mr. Swan a lesson for the first time in his life."

"Don't try," Martha begged.

That evening there was a party in her honor. Everybody who *was* anybody in town showed up—except Hyde Swan—and Sandra had taken it for granted that he would come. Later on she heard from one of the other men present that he'd gone in to New York in his private plane . . . to see a young actress with whom he was infatuated. Sandra could have killed him . . . and then she laughed to herself, at herself, and at him. Let him go. Nevertheless her evening was ruined.

Nor did he show up the next day, or the next. Sandra stopped laughing and became utterly furious; two more days passed and she submitted herself to the indignity of calling him after spending a wild night pacing the floor in a frenzy of passion for the most perfect lover she'd ever had.

"Oh," he said carelessly over the phone, "I supposed you were one of those Hollywood ladies who get bored with a man right off the bat; I didn't intend to give you a chance to get bored with me. Come on over."

SANDRA HUMBLED HERSELF and drove over. He was all ready to play tennis when she got there; looking tempting in white flannels, which were a perfect contrast for his dark hair and eyes.

While they were having a cocktail preliminary to a tennis set Sandra asked:

"Are you really carrying on an *affaire* with Gracie Montrose; and did you really stand me up the other evening on that account?"

"Of course," he told her blithely. "Do you think I'm fool enough to let you lose interest in me by thinking no other woman is interested in me? I've been plenty hurt by women in the past; now I strike first."

"But why should you prefer a person like her to — "

"To you? Well, there are reasons, Sandra. You're better looking, cultured, altogether more provocative . . . but Gracie's not as particular as you might be. She conforms to little tricks of dalliance that would hurt or sicken you, since you're a softy."

"I'm a what?"

"Come on, let's go," he laughed. On the tennis court he drove her so hard that by the end of several sets she was in a state bordering upon collapse. While she was resting on a lounge in the living room, too tired out to slap him, he told her about some of the things Gracie would do that she wouldn't. She agreed with him and left as soon as she was able, without even kissing him. His mocking laugh followed her out the door. "Beast!" she said to herself.

But she found that Hyde Swan was not so easily disposed of. All through dinner she thought; when she went to bed she was in a delium of thought. Restlessly all night she lay awake, still thinking.

AND FROM THAT TIME on it was plain hell. Did she refuse to comply with his more painful and sickening whims, he refused to see her at all . . . the summer became a perfect torment to Sandra; yet it was shot with moments of passion that transcended anything of which she had ever dreamed; and at last, as a crowning triumph, she saw that the hard boiled Hyde Swan had fallen in love with her. Grimly she bided her time.

"I *warned* you," Martha moaned, as, despairingly she saw Sandra grow thinner, and look increasingly worried. "What on earth will you *do?* You're in love with him!"

"Do?" Sandra echoed grimly. "Watch and see."

And then one day Hyde Swan came over to the house looking sheepish.

"What's the devil's the matter?" he asked angrily. "Haven't heard from Sandra for three days."

"She's gone," Martha told him placidly.

"Gone?" he echoed blankly. "Gone without a word to me!" He was aghast. To her astonishment Martha noted his profound agitation; at last somebody had succeeded in taming the untamable Hyde.

"She left a note for you," Martha reported.

(*Please turn to page* 64)

SAILOR in LOVE

His arms went around her waist, his strong capable hands supporting her back.

By
MYRNA WILLIAMS

THE BROAD WATERS of the lower Hudson, black from the oil drippings of snub-nosed tugs and heavy with the stench of melted tar from the ferryboat docks, caught the strident moans of a hundred steam whistles from every manner of dingy river craft and hurled them back at the smoky sky with three-fold resonance.

Like a giant, grey spectre barging out of the misty pall that usually covers the lower bay, the flagship of the Atlantic Fleet, ensigns fluttering in the wind, led its long line of sleek, sea-trim charges through the water-way that separates New York and New Jersey.

"The Fleet's in!" . . . "The Fleet's in!" . . . "The Fleet's in!"

Up and down the landscaped stretches of Riverside Drive, the cry sounded. Nursemaids with their hooded carriages, boys at play, old men out for an airing, all crowded to the stone walls of the ramps, eyes turned to the engaging sight.

It was all old stuff to Terence Rafferty O'Toole, and his red, pug-nosed face showed it as he leaned against the forward rail of the third cruiser in line, the *U. S. S. Brevoort,* and gazed at the jagged edges of the New York skyline. It was old stuff, and yet, there was a certain glory in steaming up the river like a conquering hero to the accompaniment of whistles and cannon shots. Of course, Mr. O'Toole knew the whistles and cannon shots were no more intended for him than they were for Mahatma Ghandi, but still and all, he was part and parcel of the Fleet and therefore entitled to part and parcel of the welcome.

Naturally, the Admiral up on the quarterdeck of the *Kentucky* was the big shot of the day's festivities. At least, he was the big shot until the shore leave orders were given and the motor launches began shifting the boys from ship to ship. Then, New York was a sailor's playground, Admirals or no Admirals.

Even this thought failed materially to cheer Terence Rafferty O'Toole. The knowledge that the green slopes of Riverside Drive were even now dotted with sailors' sweethearts, more than enough to go around, gave him a swift pain in the neck. It was strange, this sudden aversion to being accosted by feminine pulchritude in wholesale lots, but Mr. O'Toole had reason enough for his feelings in the matter.

The physical part of that reason was back in Port au Prince, but the mental part remained with Terence, a carbuncle on his consciousness. In his mind's eye he could see her again, a hard, brown passion-flower of a girl, with slim, curving hips and jutting conical breasts that pointed up like mango gourds. He had enjoyed pronouncing her name—Renga—letting it roll off his tongue to lose its first syllable in the rumbling of his Irish brogue. He had enjoyed, too, holding her warm body in his arms and joining his lips with the soft fire of her mouth, and feeling the stabbing pressure of her bosom through his shirt.

Terence was a sailor with ideals. He had never subscribed to the "sweetheart in every port" axiom that seems to cling to the boys in blue, not without reason. Year in and year out, as the Fleet made its ports of call the varied harbors of the world, he watched his mates skip blithely from one amour to another without batting an eyelash. Under duress, Terence joined them in their wild escapades from Cristobal to Newport News, but somehow he had no heart for the game of "love 'em and leave 'em". His one dream (as yet not come to realization) was to find the girl of girls, be true to her, and when his current term of enlistment ended, leave the Navy for business and babies.

Five times, thus far, the dream had come to earth. Five times in five different climes with five different dream ladies, and a net result of five failures. Terence disliked reviewing the past, but oftentimes he would wonder why the spell hadn't lasted at least once. All of them were pretty, all of them well built and all of them eager . . . for a while. And then, he had either discovered them in another sailor's arms, found they were just waterfront parasites, or learned, to his horror, that a husband lurked in the offing.

Possessing an undercover husband was the reason for the Renga-Port au Prince affair's failing to click. True, Renga wasn't wholly white, but Terence, with typical Irish broadmindedness, drew no color line as long as there were curved thighs, boyish hips and hard, taut-skinned little breasts that resembled dwarf cocoanuts. Terence drew no color line, but the law, even in brown countries, drew a husband line.

It was not so much Renga's husband as Renga's denying that she ever possessed one that got Mr. O'Toole. He had five days shore leave in Port au Prince and spent four days and twenty-three hours of it with Renga. When the time drew close for him to return to the ship, he pressed fifty dollars in good, United States money into her damp palm and whispered something about returning in a year to marry her and take her away.

As Terence was stepping out the door, the husband stepped in. He was a big husband, towering almost six inches above the O'Toole shock of red hair, and if not for that, Terence would have made some form of protestation when Renga divided the fifty with her legal mate, went into his arms and gurgled happily as he carried her to the bed.

It was the last straw for Terence Rafferty O'Toole, and hence his bored demeanor as the *U. S. S. Brevoort* steamed in through the Narrows and came to anchor opposite Grant's Tomb. The vision of Renga, in the arms of another man, giving her lips to other lips, loomed larger on Terence's horizon than the great General's granite and limestone sepulchre. Even the flutter of white, feminine handkerchiefs on the green shore failed to arouse a responsive note in Terence's sensibilities.

"Women," he said, addressing his remarks

to a lone seagull bobbing in the water of the port side of the ship, "are no good!"

FIVE MINUTES AFTER the motor launch had deposited Terence and forty of his mates on the island the Indians were inveigled to sell for the price of two orchestra seats to the *Ziegfeld Follies,* he was strolling along the Drive, puffing absently on a cigarette. He laughed inwardly at the sublime insanity of some of his mates, leaping into the arms of waiting girls and showering them with smacking kisses. Probably the following night they would do the same thing with a sailor from the *Dakota,* or maybe the night before they did it with a Marine!

Dusk was settling over the river, and inland, the tower beacon of the Empire State Building gleamed like a monstrous diamond. Terence took long, loping strides, stretching his thigh muscles and getting back his land legs. It had been two weeks since he had set foot on terra firma and the roll of the sea was hard to forget. He turned to look back on the *Brevoort,* riding gracefully at anchor, and bumped headlong into a breathless girl coming in the other direction.

Terence's arms shot out as he realized the impact was bowling her over. They went around her waist, his strong, capable hands supporting her back. When she was righted, Terence doffed his white hat.

"I'm sorry," he said, blushing to the roots of his vivid red hair.

The girl's brown eyes sparkled. "Oh, that's all right," she panted. "I guess I wasn't looking. You see, I'm in such a hurry because I think I'm late." She seemed to notice, for the first time, that he was wearing a sailor's uniform. "Oh, you're a sail—a naval man!" she gasped. "Do you know whether all the boys are off the *Brevoort?*"

"You mustn't tell him you were out with me, understand?"

Terence gulped. Despite all the excitement, he had permitted himself the pleasure of a quick examination of the feminine half of his collision, and strangely, all the gloomy thoughts he had suffered from were rapidly being dispelled. She was of medium height with brown hair peeping from beneath a smart cloque, lustrous brown eyes that twinkled merrily, pouting, cupid's-bow lips, and a figure that was evidently full-breasted and curved beneath a tailored suit.

"Er—yes, I think the last launch-load just

landed," he replied. As a matter of sober fact, he *knew* the last launch-load had landed because he was on it.

Her brow wrinkled. "Then—then I guess I missed him, didn't I?" she queried petulantly.

"Missed who?"

"The boy I wanted to meet."

"Well, wouldn't he be waiting for you?" Terence could even imagine himself waiting for this cute trick.

"Well—er," she said hesitantly, "he—he didn't know I was coming to meet him. He—he doesn't know me."

Terence nodded. One of those blind dates. He hid his hat behind him so that she would not see the *U. S. S. Brevoort* on the starched rim.

"What's the boy's name?" he asked.

"Terence O'Toole," she replied quickly.

For a moment Terence felt like the man who visited the Taj Mahal in India and found his name scratched on a teakwood pillar. The bit of a detective in every human prompted him to remain silent for the time being.

"Do you know him?" she questioned hopefully.

Terence thought quickly. Sooner or later, if he followed out the plan he had in mind, she would see the lettered *U. S. S. Brevoort* on his white hat. Might as well spring it on her now.

"Er—yes," he said, "I—I know O'Toole. You see, I'm on the *Brevoort,* too." He brought the hat from behind his back and held it up before her.

Her eyes sparkled. "Then you know him? Is he still at the dock?"

Terence shook his head negatively. "No, lady, he isn't. I saw him hop a street car for Times Square. Guess he's goin' out on a bat tonight. O'Toole likes the ladies."

She sighed. "Oh, well, it's my fault for being late." She smiled graciously. "Thanks anyway."

Two minutes of conversation with her and Mr. O'Toole had completely forgotten Renga and her undercover husband. In fact, he had completely forgotten everything but the problem (and it was a pleasantly curved and sweet problem) that faced him.

"You're not going, are you?" he asked.

Her eyes showed surprise. "Why—er—yes. Since I missed him there's no point in hanging around. He won't come back, will he?"

Terence shrugged. "I hardly think so, lady. Once O'Toole gets ashore he stays ashore until the last minute." He paused, twirling his hat around his index finger. "But I'm here, lady," he said quietly. "Can't I substitute for O'Toole?"

He thought he detected a blush suffusing her cheeks, but possibly it was just the bloom of her delicate make-up.

"Well," she began, "I did want to meet Mr. O'Toole, but since I missed him and since I met you . . . "

Terence took her arm and slipped it into his. "Enough said, Miss . . .er . . . Miss . . . "

"Toddy Kind," she replied.

"O. K. Enough said, Toddy. Introduce yourself to Jack Riley of Uncle Sam's boys in blue and forget all about Mr. O'Toole right her and now."

She seemed to lean up against him as they walked towards Tenth Avenue, smiling into his Irish eyes. Terence was certain, as he felt the soft pressure of her hip, and looked down to the bulging symmetry of her breasts, that his luck was changing.

"You are a very fortunate young lady," he said, squeezing her round arm, "being able to swap an O'Toole for a Riley!"

She smiled quizzically, almost giving him her pouting red lips in broad daylight.

Across a table at a not too snooty restaurant, Terence studied Toddy intently, wondering what stroke of good fortune had caused him to turn his head on Riverside Drive and bump into this girl. She had removed her light Spring jacket and sat before him attired in a brown linen waist that bellied and flattened wherever firm flesh beneath it caused it to belly and flatten. The neckline, cut in a low V-shape, was fastened with a scarab pin, something like the ones Terence had seen in the open-air jewelry mart of Calcutta. He almost wished the scarab was alive and could crawl away from the junction of the two sides of the waist, permitting it to fall apart and reveal her white breasts in all their alabaster glory. From where he sat, his head inches above hers, he could look down and just glimpse the rolling curves of flesh that were the upper mounds of her bosom. From the sample he could judge the rest.

"You haven't told me why you were so anxious to meet O'Toole, Toddy," he said, trying to assume a nonchalant air.

She patted his hand. "Forget it, Jack. I'm not interested in him anymore. I'm glad I collided with you." Her brow furrowed. "But you mustn't tell him you were out with me, understand?"

Terence understood. "No, I'll never tell him," he replied. After all, there was little need of telling him! He had already been well told! But still, he was burning with curiosity. What object did she have in coming to meet him? He tried to think back and catalogue his New York acquaintances. There were three or four girls but they were just . . . well . . . "Fleet followers". There was old Mr. Aintree at the Seamen's Institute, but certainly *he* had no connection. Terence gave it up . . . temporarily. Possibly later in the evening, under the influence of various things he would get to the bottom of the mystery.

From the restaurant they walked up Broadway arm in arm, Terence drinking in the brilliancy of the night life scene, Toddy seemingly entranced with his company.

"Do you think I could come up with you for a little while?" he stammered.

"How about a little dancing?" he suggested questioningly.

Toddy nodded. "Sure. That'll be swell!"

There were other sailors in the Danceland Ballroom that night, but none so happy as Terence Rafferty O'Toole *alias* Jack Riley. In four short hours a slip of a brown-eyed girl with lush, inviting curves had pulled him from the trough of despondency to the heights of gaiety. As he whirled about the room, her soft body pressed close to him, the five unfortunate amatory incidents in his life were as far away as the Indian Sea.

He eased his right hand along her curved back, thrilling to the warmth of her flesh beneath the linen blouse.

"Having a good time, Toddy?" he queried.

She took a deep breath, forcing her firm breasts against his chest. "Gorgeous!" she breathed.

A shiver shot through Terence. His mind flashed back to Renga in Port au Prince with her hard, cocoanut-brown breasts. This was a white Renga he held in his arms, only parts of her were softer, more appealing. He hoped she did not possess another of Renga's virtues . . . a husband!

"You're not married, Toddy, are you?" he asked.

She grinned, red lips parting over pearly teeth. "Of course not, silly. What would I be doing with a husband?"

Terence smirked suggestively. "Just what every other girl does with a husband," he replied.

IT WAS TWO in the morning when Terence balanced himself against the lamp-post in front of Toddy's brownstone rooming house, and Toddy balanced herself against Terence.

From the dancehall they had gone to a Village hideaway, noted for the privacy of its curtained booths and for the potency of its cocktails. Two hours in a private booth and five cocktails apiece had cleared the air of any strangeness whatsoever. With experience that he had gleaned from five other women, Terence had found the twin objects of his quest and contacted their velvet skinned, taut-tipped curves. Toddy came to the conclusion that a curtained booth in a Greenwich Village hideaway was no place to carry the quest further. Suiting the action to the thought, she had removed Terence's hand, slipped on her tweed jacket and maneuvered him into the street. In the dark confines of a taxi, he took up where he had left off, molding her firm breasts in his hands with little adoring words of passion. In all his experience, Terence had never felt so attached to a woman on such short notice. He was convinced, beyond a shadow of a doubt, that this was his dream come true. Toddy, as though reading his thoughts, gave him her full-lipped mouth with damp eagerness, permitting his straying fingers to wander into increasingly sensitive territory.

And so, disgorged from the taxi, they stood in front of her rooming-house, both a little the worse for love and liquor.

"Do ya think—do ya think I could—I could come up for a little—hic—while?" Terence burped.

Toddy grinned acquiescence. "Sure, Jackie, sure! C'mon!"

Safe behind the locked door of Toddy's hall bedroom, Terence reached for her soft body, drawing her close. She protested weakly.

"Lemmee take this suit off, huh, Jackie? Ya mind?"

Not only did Terence not mind, but he was delighted. He looked on as she unhooked the skirt and let it slip down over her hips and fall to the floor. His eyes almost popped from his head as she pulled the waist over her shoulders and stood before him. She bent over to pick up the skirt and the shiny, white mounds projecting from her chest bobbed like huge corks.

The sight of all this beauty was too much for Terence's hearty appetite. In one stride he was beside her, folding her in his arms, burying his lips in the damp hollow between quivering hillocks of responsive flesh.

There was a couch. He recalled lifting her in his arms and feeling the glove-silk of her panties rub against his left palm. The next thing he knew she was in his arms, her scented lips hovering over his.

AN ELECTRIC CLOCK on the mantelpiece chimed four times as Terence stirred uneasily and pulled his numb arm from beneath Toddy's damp back.

The street lamp cast a glow through the window and across her face. Terence sighed heavily. This was the real thing; the ultimate thrill he had always looked for. Now, how to tell her he was Terence Rafferty O'Toole; how to make her understand that he was violently in love with her; how to hear from her own lips that she would wait until his enlistment period was up . . . to marry him.

She turned on her side and nestled her head in the hollow of his shoulder.

"Toddy," he whispered softly.

"Yes, darling," she murmured.

"You never—you never told me how you happened to be looking for O'Toole," he said.

She smiled in the dark. "You won't ever tell him if I tell you?" she queried.

Terence cupped a warm breast. "No, never."

"Well," she began, "one of the girls he went out with a couple of years ago told me—told me—"

(*Please turn to page* 63)

BEAUTY CONTEST

BY

KEN COOPER

OF ALL the organizers who organized things on the street that has its beginning in the shadow of the Statue of Liberty, and its end somewhere in the wilds of upper New York, and calls itself *Broadway*, Jimmy Delaney was admittedly the peer. Even high-class organizers like H. Audrey Millar, who went in for Grand Opera Benevolent Associations admitted, reluctantly, that Jimmy Delaney was gifted with the spark of organization genius.

Of course, as H. Audrey Millar pointed out, Jimmy's promotional scope was limited. He lacked social background, *savoir faire*, and the ability to win his way into the charmed circle of upper-crust society.

Strangely, these shortcomings were advantages in Jimmy Delaney's sparkling, ever-on-the-alert eyes. He would rather, any day, organize and promote a non-stop spaghetti eating contest or a jigging marathon or a peanut rolling race from City Hall to Bangor, Maine, than publicize some society debutante's coming out party.

Jimmy was lounging in the not-too-pretentious office of Al Freedman, some time theatrical broker and press agent. Physically, Jimmy was lounging, but mentally he was giving full and intensive appreciation to a pile of photographs Al Freedman had smirkingly offered for his approval.

The photographs originated in the studios of a picture taker across the hall, and were likenesses of burlesque performers and variety artists.

He held up one particularly enticing photograph of a particularly enticing female, the better to study various angles of its unadorned display. The girl was attractive in a sensual fashion. Tall and plentifully endowed, a wealth of platinum blonde hair crowned her white, high-breasted figure, vying for attention with large blue eyes and a full, too-passionate mouth. But it was not the eyes, nor the mouth, nor the platinum hair that Jimmy centered his attention on. Rather, it was the firm hillocks projecting from her upper torso, the two rotund, taut-skinned mounds bedecked with chips of clouded quartz, and seeming to invite dalliance with inarticulate forcefulness.

"Not bad at all," he commented idly, directing his opinion at Al Freedman and a ukulele player who was in to see whether Mr. Freedman knew of any places where a ukulele player could play a ukulele and get paid for it.

"What's not bad?" Mr. Freedman queried.

Jimmy tossed the platinum blonde (that is, her likeness) on Mr. Freedman's desk. "That's not bad," he said.

Mr. Freedman looked at the picture, rubbed the black bristles on the end of his chin and nodded agreement. Suddenly he looked up at the ukulele player as though he had discovered in him a second Cliff Edwards.

"All right, all right!" he barked excitedly, "I'll see if I can find something for you. Call me in a day or two."

The twanger of strings stood up with a dazed smile. Al Freedman's almost hearty invitation to call in a day or two was a bolt out of the blue. He backed out of the office murmuring profuse thanks.

When he had gone, Al turned to Jimmy, nervous fingers clutching the photograph.

"Jimmy!" he gasped nervously. "I got an idea!"

Mr. Delaney looked up casually, quitting a rather flabby lady without too much reluctance. "You always get ideas, Al, but they die from lack of nourishment," he drawled.

The theatrical booker took the affront without the flicker of an eyelash. "This is a honey, Jimmy!" he exclaimed. "Lookin' at this strip artist give me the idea." He leaned across the desk and extended one hand for emphasis. "With your ability as a promoter and my knowledge of the theatrical business," he began, but Jimmy interrupted.

"And whose money?" he queried.

Al snorted. "We won't need any money. This idea is a cinch! It's so perfect I think I should copyright it."

Jimmy sighed. "All right, go ahead. Shoot it to me."

Al took a deep breath, shifted the chewed mass of what once was a fairly respectable five-cent cigar from the left side of his face to the right and launched into his story.

"Do you know what they got in Galveston, Texas, every year?" he demanded, almost arrogantly.

"No," he replied, "what have they got in Galveston, Texas, every year, Al?"

Mr. Freedman waved his hand in a deprecating manner. "No, nothing like that," he exclaimed. "My idea is even bigger, more ambitious." He swelled his chest and flashed three gold-capped front teeth. "My idea is to bring the International Beauty Contest to New York and run it ourselves." He leaned back confidently, waiting for the reaction. It came, sooner than he expected.

"Then that means I'm in the contest, Mr. Delaney?" she baby-talked.

Al beamed. "A beauty contest!" he exclaimed. "An International Beauty Contest!"

Jimmy shuffled the pictures in his hands. "I got that right here," he countered, "only most of them are muggs."

The agent made a disgusted noise with his lips. "Those are just dogs," he said, "but my idea is—"

"To go down to Galveston, Texas, with a couple of girls and cop all the prizes," Jimmy supplied. "I'm way ahead of you, Al, way ahead!" It was Jimmy's pride and joy to be ahead of people, particularly people who wore a badge or carried a warrant.

"Sure," Jimmy agreed, "that's a swell idea, Al. So is the idea some guy had of floating the Empire State Building and renting out the offices to fishermen. Or another good idea would be to move Central Park to the middle of the Atlantic Ocean and use it to grow spinach."

For long moments, Mr. Al Freedman failed to appreciate the subtle sarcasm. Finally it hit him, right between the eyes. "So, you think it can't be done, huh?" he sneered. "Well, if they can do it in a jerkwater town like Galveston, Texas, we can do it in New York."

Jimmy was on the point of losing his patience, but he found it and tucked it back where it belonged. "Al," he said quietly, "do you know what the word *International* means?"

Al shrugged. "I shouldn't know? Of course I know. It means all the countries."

Jimmy raised his hand. "Well, if *International* means every country, how in hell do you expect to get girls from every country for a beauty contest? In Galveston, Texas, the Board of Trade underwrites the contest and pays the beauty winners in each country to come over. It'll take at least ten thousand in cash. Have you got it?"

Mr. Freedman's face went a trifle blank. Assuredly he did not have ten thousand dollars or the remotest part of it. As a matter of fact and record he had, a scant ten minutes ago, planned on touching Jimmy for the price of a corned beef sandwich and a glass of tea. He chewed on the already well-chewed cigar with cannibalistic savagery. There must be some way out of it. His face brightened.

"I got it! I got it!" he yelled.

"You got what?"

"A solution! A swell solution to the problem! Where is it written that these girls must be *born* in the countries they're supposed to come from, hah? Where is it written that a girl couldn't come over here from, let's say, Italy, when she was two years old, and still be an Eyetalian girl, hah? I ask you, where is it written?"

Jimmy held his peace, mulling the matter over in his mind. There *was* something in what Freedman said! He remembered *Miss New York* for 1932, partly because he had tried to promote her into posing for Slendawate Reducing Cream and partly because she was well worth remembering. As he recalled, now that Al brought the point up, *Miss New York* was born, raised and lived in Hoboken, New Jersey.

Mr. Freedman waited a reasonable time for a response. Finally he grew impatient. "Well?" he queried. "Well?"

Jimmy nodded. "I see *your* point, Al," he said, trying to find a point that would put him way ahead of his friend. "New York is a melting pot. Girls of all nationalities come in at its ports. Dress them up in native costumes, make them talk like foreigners, and you've got a beauty contest."

Al bobbed his head like a jack-in-the-box. "Yeah! That's right! That's right!" he cried. "Just like I pictured it." The rich, warm thrill of achievement was coursing through his veins. "I could get Moe Goodman to give me the Bronx Boxing Arena on a percentage basis. I could get a couple of swell lookin' dames to be the American entries. I could—"

Jimmy reached out for the photograph of the platinum blonde houri who possessed the exciting mammary charms. In his mind's eye he could see fifty like her parading before him to be judged.

"O. K.," he said. "We'll do it?"

IT MUST BE SAID of Jimmy Delaney that once the bug of a promotional scheme bit him, the bite was lasting. In three hectic days he had the pulse of Broadway quickening with the beauty contest idea. It would mean (according to Jimmy) an influx of out-of-town visitors, increased amusement business and a gold-mine for hotels and restaurants. Even the columnists took it up with interest.

And soon there were photographs, too, lots of them. Photographs of Jimmy, asking the Mayor to act as a judge; photographs of Jimmy sending phony cables to every country in the world, and photographs of Jimmy talking to a stunning, dark-eyed girl in an Egyptian outfit. The caption had her as Ilya Chakel, but her mother and father on Third Avenue called her Ida.

As can be well imagined, Mr. James Delaney was in his element, wading around neck deep. There was publicity, there were girls and soon there would be money. Moe Goodman had agreed to let them have the Bronx Boxing Arena for twenty per cent of the gate. The judging would be held on three nights to accommodate the big crowd. Each night a semi-finalist would be picked and if there was enough money in the till by then, the final award would be made at Madison Square Garden before twenty thousand people at a dollar a head.

Al Freedman's job was to round up the girls for Jimmy's approval. For the first time in his life he found it necessary to go out after performers rather than have them come in to him. From every source he collected them, until fully four hundred names were filed in his office.

Trouble has a way of beginning pleasantly. In this case the trouble that reared its ugly head to menace the International Beauty Contest Association began so pleasantly that it no more resembled trouble than a lima bean resembles Mae West. It began (as trouble always does) with a woman. It reached gigantic proportions because of two women. It landed on the International Beauty Contest Association like a ton of bricks because of *three* women!

The first woman in the picture had blonde hair, blue eyes and a figure that almost approached dumpiness, but just managed somehow to sneak by with the description "plump". Her name was Betty Bachrach and she came from Canarsie, which, as anybody knows, is where people try not to come from.

When Jimmy set eyes on Betty from Canarsie, he thought the beauty contest business was one of the best businesses in the world. Betty was attired in an ecru silk dress, one size too small for her, but calculated to bring out every hill and valley of her body with faithful perfection. To say that it fulfilled its mission would be to put it mildly. From Betty's white throat to her acceptable ankles, the road the eye had to travel was up hill and down dale, broken by veritable precipices of breasts, jutting forth like formidable sentries guarding the cute rotundity of her "tummy" below.

Jimmy studied her as she posed before him, exerting all the come-hither qualities of her eyes and all the physical appeal of her voluptuous body. He smiled approvingly and nodded to Al Freedman.

"A swell Swedish type," he said.

Al, unaffected by the display of feminine attributes which had paraded in and out his dingy office for the last ten years, nodded. "Yeah," was his only comment.

Betty sidled over to Jimmy, undulating her hips with practiced seduction. "Then that means I'm in the contest, Mister Delaney?" she baby-talked.

Jimmy grinned. "That's what it means, baby. A chance for you to cop anywhere from fifty to a thousand bucks just for parading around a wooden platform."

Betty was from Canarsie, which is slightly different from Missouri, chiefly because in Canarsie girls do not have to be shown . . . they already know!

"Is that *all* I'll have to do, Mister Delaney?" she questioned, pouting her red lips.

Jimmy noted that Al was engaged in conversation with a booking agent friend. "Well," he said, "if there's anything else you can do *well,* you might tip me off."

She raised herself on tip-toes and lifted her face up to him. Jimmy glanced down and the sight that met his eyes clinched his grand opinion of beauty contests once and for all. The ecru silk dress was tight about Betty's figure, particularly in the region of her plentiful breasts, but the neckline was not too tight to hide the indentation between the heavy hillocks; an indentation that was downy, shadowed and darkly intriguing.

"Everything I do, I do well, Mister Delaney," she whispered.

They had dinner together at Joe's Blue Room, and when that was finished went to a movie, and when that was finished, Jimmy turned to Betty.

"Now what?" he questioned, just as a matter of form.

Betty smiled. "Oh, a little roller skating in the park or a motor dash to Miami, I guess." She squeezed his arm, still palpitant from the contact of his hand on her thigh in the dark movies. "Where's your hotel?"

In the hotel room, she threw all caution to the four winds and flung her arms about Jimmy's neck, melting her plump body to his with intoxicating nearness.

"Kiss me, Jimmy!" she pleaded, breathless.

Jimmy kissed her, and by some miracle the shoulder straps of her dress began to slip, and in another moment, the entire garment was in a heap on the floor. A lace brassiere and a ridiculously abbreviated pair of panties constituted Betty's only other covering and it was scant covering indeed.

Later, hours later, Betty's husky voice broke the silence. "We know who's going to win the beauty contest, don't we, Jimmy?"

Jimmy sighed, his body suffused with the warmth of hers. "Yes, darling," he whispered.

THE SECOND WOMAN in the picture came from Greenwich Village and her name was Sonya. She was Russian—*really* Russian—but not the Nordic Russian. Her ebony hair was parted in the center and drawn down in a tight bun at the nape of her neck. Her skin was dead white and her mouth a bloody gash in the pallor. Her eyes were brown, heavy lidded and long-lashed, boding no good for any man, least of all, Jimmy Delaney.

Sonia was built along lines that writers of exotic stories are inclined to call, "svelte". Her legs were long and beautiful, her thighs were round with the impression of flatness and flat with the impression of roundness, her hips curved in boyish femininity and her breasts just managed to make a cup-like impression on the bodice of any dress she wore. Sonya was no Amazonian Venus, heavy-breasted, full-hipped and sensual. Sonya was a lithe, slinky thing whose charm was all in her slinkiness and litheness.

Jimmy caught the volcanic message of her eyes, glanced at the thrilling immaturity of her breasts and catapulted. A too-strenuous diet of Betty from Canarsie was partly responsible. He was like a man who had been gorging himself on pigs knuckles and sauerkraut, and now, for a change, wanted *filet mignon.*

In his hotel room, he held her close, his hands laving the youthful hardness of her body, his lips skipping from charm to charm with passionate glee. Sonya was like light wine, sparkling and heady.

"I will win the beauty contest?" she murmured, hours later.

"It's not fair," she said. "I was promised the first prize."

Jimmy reached for her in the dark. "Of course, sweet," he replied.

THE THIRD AND LAST woman was red-headed and tough. She breezed into Al Freedman's office like a Kansas tornado, her prominent breasts jiggling jelly-like beneath her dress.

"I'm Kay Winters," she announced in a deep, throaty voice. "Which one of you is Jimmy Delaney?"

Jimmy was smitten right there and then. The very ribald lustiness of Kay Winters was something he knew he had to add to his diet.

"I'm Mr. Delaney," he said.

The red-headed hoyden flashed him a white-toothed smile. "Swell, Jimmy, I was hoping it was you." She came closer, hands on curved hips, the material of her dress pulled tight across her un-brassiered breasts. She looked handled, practiced, but it was just what Jimmy seemed to think he needed.

It was just what Kay seemed to think he needed, too, but in the hotel room she was the aggressor. Jimmy willingly submitted to the schooled intensity of her ardor. The contact of her ripe, bee-stung lips was a searing flame. Jimmy was putty in the hands of

Kay Winters, but he loved the way she modeled putty!

THE BRONX BOXING ARENA was jammed to the rafters the first night of the International Beauty Contest. After the judging, there would be dancing and entertainment furnished by the *Al Freedman Offices*. The fifty odd girls had been carefully coached and well costumed. There were Japs, Chinese, Russians, Indians, Spaniards, Italians, Swedes, and dozens of others. The four judges; a theatrical producer, a song-and-dance-man, an artist, and Jimmy Delaney, eyed the entrants as they passed by. The crowd roared, the band played and Jimmy could see success in the offing.

When the last girl had passed, the judges went into secret conclave. The opinion seemed to be unanimous. *Miss Canada*, a slim, auburn-tressed girl, a last-minute entrant, was the winner for the night. Jimmy stepped forward to the microphone.

"Ladeez and gentlemen," he began. "The winner for this evening's judging is none other than *Miss Canada!*"

The audience shouted its approval as the girl stepped forward. Jimmy eyed her round bosom beneath a white bathing suit and made a mental note to have a "chat" with her later in the evening, but the next thing that happened caused him to forget all mental and physical notes he had ever made. The microphone was snatched from his hand, a shock of red hair waved like a Russian flag and a deep, throaty voice boomed out a message to the crowd.

"It's all a fake!" the voice shouted. "None of us comes from foreign countries. Delaney is a fake and the whole contest is a fake!"

As Jimmy looked on, dazed, the microphone changed hands and a dumpy blonde was speaking into it. "I repeat what has just been said!" she shouted. "It's all a fake!"

Jimmy tried to reach the microphone but a mob of half nude girls milled about him. Now a slim, dark-haired girl in a Russian costume had the floor. "It is crooked," she said. "I was promised the first prize by Mr. Delaney. I come from Greenwich Village and *not* Russia!"

Jimmy had heard enough from the lips of Kay, Betty and Sonya to make him appreciate the need for a hasty exit. He dashed down the aisle in the direction of the box office, but veered away from the cubby-hole when he saw three burly headquarters men guarding the door. He thought, for a fleeting moment of Al Freedman and the round-breasted Miss Canada with whom he would have loved to have had a *"chat"* but a glimpse of fifty odd beauty contestants bearing down on him dispelled all thoughts. Out the door he flew and into the night.

In a restaurant in Briarwood, Nevada, Jimmy Delaney, promoter extraordinary and organizer par excellence, eyed the comely waitress between forkfulls of baked beans. Even in her starched, white uniform, she showed promise of possessing touch-provoking bosom and lissome thighs. When she came over to take his order for dessert, Jimmy opened up, deciding that a *"chat"* with her would not be too hard to take.

"You're much too good-looking to be slinging hash," he said. "I could put you on the stage or in the movies."

The waitress smiled. "I tried that, mister, but it didn't work. You see, I won a beauty contest—"

For months after, the comely waitress told the story of how the good-looking man gulped, stared at her like a maniac and dashed for the door, never to be seen again.

HEART BALM

By LOUISE LANGDON

PART TWO

THE guarded tap-tap-tap of Larry Murdock's knuckles brought instant response. The doorknob turned cautiously, and luminous blue eyes peered at him.

"How are you now?" he asked, with a friendly grin.

"All right, thanks . . . still a bit nervous, though." The girl's hand was shaking as she raised a cigarette to her tremulous lips, and her voice throbbed emotionally. Turning away, she walked to the window. The torn nightgown had been discarded for lounging pajamas, fastidiously moulding the exquisite contours of slender hips and the delightfully round globes of her breasts.

Larry accepted the fact that she had left the door ajar as a silent invitation for him to enter. He pushed it wider, stepped in, and closed it behind him.

"I thought you'd come back!" she smiled, blushing prettily.

"Why not?" he retorted. "But I hope I'm not butting in."

"On the contrary, I'm glad you came!" she assured him, pleasantly. "I wanted a chance to tell you how much I appreciate your kindness. I couldn't talk with Mrs. McGuire and all those other people around."

"Happy to have helped!" he said, airily.

"I remember screaming and dashing into the hall," she continued, "but nothing more until I found myself back in bed with you standing over me . . . I must have fainted."

"Correct!" he agreed. "So I carried you in here."

Her blush deepened. Vividly, she recalled the torn nightgown, and realized that all her sweet charms had undoubtedly been paraded before this good looking young man. . . . And he had *carried* her in . . . he had held her in his arms . . . like that!

Standing at the window, with her back to him, she plucked at her pajama jacket, seeking to arrange its folks so that it wouldn't present her breasts *quite* so attractively. . . . Men were susceptible to such things, she thought, and this one might be no exception to the rule. . . . She began to scold herself for letting him come in. . . . It was too brazen. . . . She could have talked to him for a few minutes at the door, thanked him cordially and then dismissed him. . . . After all, he was a stranger!

But it was too late to think of that now. He was in the room, and the door was shut, and he was speaking:

"Didn't go back to sleep, did you?"

"Oh, I couldn't." She glanced out of the window. "I was too nervous in the dark, but I'll try to sleep after it's daylight." She moved to the bed, sitting down and crossing her knees daintily. "Dreams are scary sometimes, aren't they?"

His eyes held her glance. "Yeah!" he drawled. "But it's much worse when it really isn't a dream."

"What do you mean?" She looked startled. "Don't you believe me?"

"Listen, girlie!" He drew up a chair, facing her. "I think that explanation about a dream was just a bit of salve for Mrs. McGuire. I encouraged her to believe it, because I knew you didn't want to frighten her. But you're too sensible a girl to let a mere dream upset you as much as that. You can be frank with me. It wasn't a dream, was it?"

Larry had decided to make a bold play for the facts. If the girl insisted that it was only a nightmare, then that was the end of it. A simple dream, however terrifying, doesn't make a newspaper story. But if the hunch in his subconscious mind wasn't wrong . . . if the girl talked frankly . . . something "hot" in the way of news might be developed.

He tried to forget the youthful beauty of the fascinatingly blonde vision sitting opposite him, her timorous attitude, her evident desire to avoid publicity. . . . He told himself that, first of all, he was a reporter, and he had to look at things impersonally and dispassionately.

In view of her previous statement, her reaction to his very pointed question was astonishingly unevasive. Prettily curling lashes curtained the violet-blue of her eyes, and she seemed to be studying the toe of a chic slipper. Then she squarely met his gaze.

"You're right!" she murmured, simply.

"Of course, it wasn't any dream. A man was in this room a while ago."

"I thought so!" said Larry, intently. "A friend of yours?"

For the first time he detected a frigidly haughty note in her voice as she replied, apparently shrinking from the implication contained in the suggestion. "Certainly not!" she declared. "I'm not in the habit of entertaining men friends in my bedroom."

"I'm sorry!" Larry hastened to make amends. "You misunderstood me."

"I was sleeping," she went on, ignoring the remark, "when a noise in the room awakened me. As I opened my eyes, I saw faintly the shadow of a man bending over a drawer of my bureau. I screamed, and then he jumped to the bed and grabbed me, clapping his hand on my mouth, but I struggled and managed to break away from him." She shuddered. "That was when I rushed out in the hall, I guess."

She lighted another cigarette. "He must have gone down the fire escape, as the window was open."

"Same way he came up, I suppose!" commented Larry. "Just another sneak thief who tried to silence you when you woke up."

"It was much more than that!" she whispered.

Larry pricked up his ears. "Did you recognize the man?"

She nodded. "He was my husband's chauffeur."

"Your husband's chauffeur!" echoed Larry. He was certain, then, that the incident had the germ of a news story. Here was a girl living in a boarding house, ostensibly alone, yet she had a husband who was wealthy enough to have a chauffeur to drive him around!

The girl's face blanched, and she swayed on the bed. Larry caught her arm to steady her, and at the same time drew a flask from his hip pocket. "Here! Take a nip of this!" he said. "It's excellent brandy, and it'll steady your nerves."

She pushed his hand away. "No, thanks! I'll be all right."

Heaving a tired sigh, her expanding chest caused the lovely minarets of her breasts to be sketched below her pajamas so lusciously that Larry's interest would have been vastly intrigued if he had been viewing her as a pretty girl instead of an impersonal source of news!

"I don't know why I'm telling you all this!" she murmured. "You've probably got troubles of your own, without bothering yourself with my affairs."

"Go ahead!" he urged. "Maybe I can help you." He slipped the flask into his pocket again.

"Oh, never mind . . . it'll all blow over, I guess." She smiled across at him. "Now you'd better be getting back to your room. Old Mrs. McGuire might be rather peevish if she discovered you here again."

"Let me worry about that!" he laughed. "I'm like one of those knight errants of the long ago, always ready to rescue a damsel from the clutches of a villainous ogre! . . . Go on, please; . . . Tell me about yourself."

Her heart warmed to him. He gave the impression of being so very trustworthy, so level-headed and self-confident! She longed to confide in somebody.

"Well, if you insist . . . " she began. "I'm June Watson. Perhaps you've heard of the Pittsburgh Watsons . . . socially prominent, wealthy . . . Carton Watson, their youngest son, was my husband."

Larry felt like whistling gleefully. He was on the track of news. The Watsons were in the upper-crust of society. He remembered the story about the rash elopement of young Carter, so this girl must be the pretty chorine in the case! Larry could visualize the headlines: *"Millionaire's Ex-Bride Attacked By Chauffeur!"*

"Carter Watson's parents were furious with him for marrying me," June continued, "and we were divorced a few months ago, after they forced him to leave me by threatening to disinherit him. A separation agreement was signed, and he guaranteed to do certain things which haven't been done. His folks were doubly angry because he signed the agreement, and he would do anything in the world to get it back from me."

Larry smiled. "That's what the tabloid newspapers would call a heart-balm contract!" he observed.

"Oh, don't misunderstand me!" she said. "I'm not interested in his money, or alimony, or anything like that. . . . If he isn't man enough to carry out his agreement, he needn't do anything about it, because I won't force him, but he can at least quit trying to steal the contract by underhanded methods!"

Larry admired the way she tossed her blonde curls defiantly.

"I've been moving around from house to house every week or so, trying to avoid him, but that chauffeur of his shadows me wher-

ever I go. This is the third time this month that he has tried to rob me of my copy of that contract. I took this room only yesterday, and tonight you know what happened." Her voice trailed off in a whisper.

"You should have told the police!" advised Larry.

"I didn t want any publicity!" she replied. "If the newspapers were tipped off, there would be plenty of headlines and my life would be even more miserable with reporters and photographers."

Larry coughed. She must have forgotten, in her excitement, all about the fact that she had been told he was a newspaperman when she recovered from her fainting spell. If she only knew that his interest in her was originally motivated by the scent of a news story! And that story was rapidly developing into something worth while! He felt the prickings of a guilty conscience.

"This Carter Watson is a bad egg isn't he?" asked Larry.

"I thought he was all right, but he turned out to be the reverse." She sighed plaintively.

"I've heard rumors about him." Larry got off his chair, strolled to the window and glanced out at the graying dawn. "He's been mixed up in some rather shady deals, and he'd be in jail if it weren't for his folks' money and influence. How did you come to marry him?"

"I was on the stage when I met him," replied June. "I was crazy about him at first, and thought he really loved me." A pink flush was mantling her throat.

"There's a proverb, girlie, about marrying in haste and repenting at leisure!" Larry had found out about all he needed to know for his sensational story. In the back of his mind, he was already trying to devise a way to keep June's name and address out of it. Her name was not so important, anyway. It was Carter Watson who made it news!

"By the way," said Larry, "what's the chauffeur's name?"

She knit her brows. "It's a peculiar name . . . Tony something . . . I never could remember his last name."

"Not Tony Dominico?" He paused waiting for her reply.

"Yes, that's it?" she smiled. "Or isn't it? . . . I'm sure of it, the way you pronounce it, although I couldn't get it right."

Larry was amazed. . . . Luck was running his way. . . . He was uncovering a story of the first magnitude. . . . Tony Dominico was Carter Watson's private chauffeur . . . Tony the Greek! . . . Gunman, gangster, dope-smuggler and small time bootlegger . . . a man who would do anything for a price! . . . He was the man who was mixed up in the narcotic case that Larry had just been mainly instrumental in solving. . . . The authorities were hunting Tony, high and low, certain that his capture would lead to the discovery of the man who was financing the ring! . . . Tony's boss!

June noticed Larry's perturbed reaction to her announcement. "What's the matter? Do you know Tony?"

"I've had reports about him, and he isn't a very nice person." He laughed cynically. "Where's Carter Watson now?"

"He went to Europe with his folks a couple of weeks ago. It was in the papers." June's big blue eyes were staring at him. She was leaning back against a pillow now, one shapely leg tucked under her, the other dangling over the edge of the bed, delicious crescents of breasts peeking from the yoke of her pajamas.

But there was nothing repulsive about her pose or in her shining eyes, and Larry felt instinctively that she was *different* from other girls he knew or had known. . . . He wanted to sweep her into his arms and kiss that rosy-red mouth, now that masculine instincts were predominating over the coldly calculating mental processes of the newspaperman, but he controlled himself with an effort.

"Maybe I *can* help you!" he said, strolling over to the door. "I'll roll the situation around in my mind. In the meantime, try to get some sleep and, remember, no more dreams!" He grinned boyishly.

June laughed. "Thanks a lot!"

Larry's last glimpse of her was hauntingly attractive, curled up on the bed like a pink and white and gold kitten!

ONCE MORE HE TROD the stairs on the way up to his room. He had completely forgotten his weariness, and in its stead a spirit of exultant triumph possessed him. His "nose for news" hadn't played him false. All he had to do now was to verify a few facts, and then he would be able to write a story that would be certain to carry a sensational headline!

And what a girl was June! "Sweet kid!" he thought. "Just the sort of a girl I'd like to marry . . . if I ever thought of getting married . . . and fancy a girl as nice as June falling for such a sappy guy as that

Carter Watson . . . well, we all make mistakes . . . "

Thoughtfully musing, with downcast eyes, he didn't see Daisy's lush contours framed in the doorway of her room until he heard a voice, in a taunting lilt, say:

"You're a naughty boy!"

Larry smiled. "Are you still up? Don't you ever go to bed and stay there?"

Daisy was known as the girl with "bedroom eyes". . . . It was a fitting description. . . . Large, heavy-lidded, tigerish eyes they were, and every glance said a silent invitation: "*Come-play-with-me*" . . . One of those eyes winked knowingly at Larry.

"I might ask you the same question!" she murmured. "You seem to be commuting between the second and third floors. Didn't you remind me a while ago that Mrs. McGuire didn't permit promiscuous visiting?"

Her red hair blazed like a prairie fire. Her silk pajamas had given way to a nightdress, and it was the thinnest garment that Larry had ever seen on a feminine form. The dawn had evolved into bright daylight, and as she stood in the doorway, the light from the window delineated her voluptuous curves as plainly as though she were unclad.

The upper portion of her nightdress might have been absent entirely, so far as coverage went . . . just a bit of lace above her waist, and the breasts that were being exhibited for Larry's benefit were amazing mounds of soft delight, challenging a caress. . . . There wasn't a thing about her which didn't suggest the experience of sophistication and the passionate yearning of an amorous soul.

"I can't blame you, Larry Murdock . . . she's pretty!" continued Daisy. "Did you have a good time, darling?" She raised a rounded arm to capture a straying lock of hair and wind it behind her ear. "I saw the girl when she came in yesterday afternoon. Tell me, can she kiss as well as she can scream?"

"I'm surprised at you, Daisy!" he said, laughing. "I only went down to see if she was okay."

"Yeah!" said Daisy, dreamily. "That's what they all say."

"Go on back to bed!" he said.

"With my dreams?" she murmured. "If I did dream, though, I wouldn't scream, Larry darling . . . I'd only sigh!"

Larry would have been less than human if he hadn't experienced a disturbing thrill viewing and listening to this tigerish creature at arm's length.. . . . Waves of an oriental perfume, headily pungent came from her.

"Your husband ought to be here to take care of you!" he remarked.

"Undoubtedly!" she retorted. "But, you see, he isn't here, and that should mean something to you . . . or doesn't it?"

"It means that you should be sleeping alone!" countered Larry.

"But that's not what I mean!" Daisy shot back. "Your friend on the second floor, who screams so wildly in the middle of the night, is a very pretty blonde. . . . But haven't you any time for a red-head who is also wild, and, incidentally, very willing?"

Larry's feet shuffled uneasily. He glanced about the hall, listening intently. The house was silent. He had that nice, tired feeling . . . the kind that welcomes soft arms intertwining, a softly warm body pressed in close embrace, a moist mouth clinging passionately, a melting sigh!

Daisy seized his hand, lacing her fingers with his.

"Are you very sleepy?" she whispered.

"I ought to be!" he answered.

"So should I, but I'm not!" She chuckled. She was pulling him ever closer to her, guiding the hand she held so that his arm would encircle her pliant waist.

"Let's smoke a cigarette together!" she breathed.

"I've done nothing but smoke for three days!" he said. His voice was growing husky.

"Then one more cigarette will never hurt you!" she urged.

Gradually, irresistibly, she had pulled him across the threshold of the doorway. The light at the head of her bed had been extinguished. It wasn't necessary any longer. The sun was peeping through the window!

"All right!" he said. "Light me one, will you?"

The door shut noiselessly. Daisy crossed to her bureau, plucked two cigarettes from a package, struck a match and lighted first one, then the other.

"Sit down, Larry!" she murmured, pushing him over to the bed. "You seem to be so nervous. . . . What's wrong? . . . Afraid of Mrs. McGuire?"

She glided over to him, pressing the tip of a lighted cigarette to his lips. . . . Her fingertips were perfumed, too, he noticed, and a silky leg contacted his knee.

"Best time of day, the dawn!" she whis-

(*Please turn to page* 63)

Personal Chauffeur

By

FRANK KENNETH YOUNG

THE PHONE RANG in the Maitland garage. Don West dropped the magazine he was reading, and moved to answer the summons.

Mrs. Maitland's voice came musically over the wire: "I have decided to go shopping. Bring the Chrysler around, please."

Hanging up the receiver, Don turned to one of the three luxurious cars which it was his duty to keep ready for instant use. He sprang into the drivers seat, and pressed the starter.

The motor purred smoothly. The car—a beautiful "Airflow" design—seemed to float down the ramp and out into the gravel drive. Making a graceful half turn, it slid to a smooth stop in front of the Maitland residence.

Don glanced at the gas gauge, and leaned back to wait. . . .

Although a professional chauffeur, he was not in livery. Mrs. Maitland was of democratic mind. She had protested against his wearing anything that might even suggest uniform.

"Dress plainly but neatly," she had instructed, when taking Don into her employ. "I dislike the idea of riding behind a man in livery. It makes me feel as though I were part of a parade!"

Don had been glad to dispense with the trick costume.

He was now attired in a natty suit of gray tweeds, with cloth cap to match, soft silk shirt and dark blue tie. He was handsome, stalwart, manly. One might easily have mistaken him for the owner of the car. . . .

The door of the house opened, and Mrs. Maitland emerged upon the verandah. Don sprang to the ground and opened the car door.

Another of Mrs. Maitland's rules was that he was always to behave like a human being and not like an automaton. She had instructed him to avoid all forms of stiff-backed artificiality, such as were usually affected by factotums.

"Be yourself!" she had said. "Gentlemanly, courteous, efficient, obedient! But, for heaven's sake, don't stand rigidly at attention when I'm giving instructions, or act like a frozen-faced marble statue and gaze straight through me or over my head! I won't have it! . . . "

Accordingly, Don turned to gaze, this morning, at the lady as she descended the steps.

And, as always, he was both impressed and thrilled by her appearance. She was his idea of a Perfect Matron—past the "newlywed" age, still far from the "middle" age, at just the right stage of womanly maturity!

She was wearing an adorable hat and an expensive street dress. Don didn't know much about such things. He was impressed by the way they became the wearer, rather than by style or actual design. He only knew that Mrs. Maitland's garments always fit her to the well-known "T", and seemed a natural complement to her beauty. . . .

She nodded brightly and said: "Good morning, Don! You are prompt, I see—and that is the one virtue that I admire most of all!"

Don replied: "Thank you, Ma'am! I trust you will find the car in good condition . . . "

MRS. MAITLAND always hitched her dress a trifle higher before placing her foot upon the step. She did so this morning. And Don, who stood ready to assist her to the seat inside, was given a brief glimpse of dainty slipper, neatly-turned ankle, and a portion of a silk-dressed calf.

This morning, as always when she leaned forward, her matronly breasts swung slightly forward in the loose, low front of her dress, and Don saw a delightful expanse of pink-and-white flesh swelling into two luscious mounds, and the beginning of a triangular valley, deep, mysterious and enchanting.

As she climbed inside, his gaze swept appreciatively over her bowed back, and lingered for a second longer than was necessary upon the curves of voluptuous hips and thighs, with the street dress drawn snugly about them.

Mrs. Maitland had a most seductive figure. Her attractive curves were more than surplus flesh. Her shoulders were broad; her back was tapering; her hips were well-formed, well-proportioned. . . .

Don waited patiently in front of behind the wheel. Gazing into the rear-view mirror, he saw Mrs. Maitland settle herself comfortably, with little wriggling movements that disturbed her full-fleshed bosom.

"Stop first at Parker's," she instructed. "I shall want to shop there . . . "

Don waited patiently in front of Parker's, while the lady did her shopping, and was somewhat surprised when, presently, she appeared with a friend whom she had met in the store.

"I'm driving Mrs. Faulkner home," she explained. "Go around by her house."

As Don assisted both ladies into the car, he observed that Mrs. Faulkner was every bit as lovely as his employer, and of about the same age. Then he closed the door and climbed into the front seat.

As he drove slowly along, the ladies chattered volubly, and he could not help overhearing scraps of their low-toned conversation. . . .

"Only twenty-four fifty, and the duckiest little panties you ever saw!" Mrs. Faulkner was saying. "I can hardly wait till I get them on! Imported black lace, interwoven with rose-colored silk ribbons. Reinforced in front and rear, of course; but web-like on both sides, so that the white flesh of the hips will show in striking contrast!"

"Beautiful!" exclaimed Mrs. Maitland. "Your husband will go crazy when he sees you in them!"

"There's a V-brassiere to match," Mrs. Faulkner continued. "Barely two lace cups held together by ribbons. I shall probably never wear it unless on special occasions. My breasts, though large and protruding, are firm and elastic enough to hold their own. I very rarely wear a brassiere unless for the sake of appearances."

"I don't like them, either," admitted Mrs. Maitland. "Yet I must wear one if I do much running around. Too much bobbing and jiggling is a strain on my bosom. Sometimes, it becomes actually painful!"

"Massage will remedy that," observed Mrs. Faulkner wisely. "You should have an affectionate boy friend, if your husband's business keeps him occupied!"

"That might help some," laughed Mrs. Maitland. Then, lowering her voice: "I've got one picked out—handsome, tall and broad-shouldered—a perfect darling!"

Mrs. Faulkner: "Who is he?"

Don's ears burned hotly. Mrs. Maitland made no oral reply. But Don sensed, without seeing, that she nodded toward him!

"Oh, my dear!" gushed Mrs. Faulkner in stage whispers. "That's marvelous! . . . Have you . . . ?"

"Not yet! I've had him in my employ only a week. I'm waiting for the opportunity to sound him out, and if he is agreeable—" She paused significantly.

"You lucky thing!" gurgled Mrs. Faulkner. "Take care, or I'll be stealing him from you! I could go for a handsome boy! . . . "

By a mighty effort, Don kept his gaze glued to the road, and his mind on his driving. But his heart was thumping furiously, and he tingled in every nerve.

A lot of silly gossip, he reflected. A couple of rattle-headed dames who talked trash because they could think of nothing sensible to say. And yet—could it be possible that Mrs. Maitland—?

He brought the car to a smooth stop in front of the Faulkner residence, and got out to open the door.

"Thank you for bringing me home," said Mrs. Faulkner.

"Don't mention it, darling!" replied Mrs. Maitland. "But, listen! There's a new Style Shoppe opening in the East End, and they are showing the latest Parisian creations! Let's go shopping again tomorrow, will you? I'll come this way and pick you up."

"Why, I'll be delighted!"

Mrs. Faulkner turned in her seat and reached out a long, curved leg, groping with her foot for the step.

For an instant, as she grasped Don's helping hand, he felt her weight upon him; then she leaped to the ground with a springy jar that caused those large, protruding mounds to bob, and he felt an extra pressure from her warm fingers.

Slipping her hand caressingly from his grasp, she spoke a few final words to Mrs. Maitland, then ran toward the house. . . .

Don climbed in behind the wheel, wondering if his employer had noticed Mrs. Faulkner's subtle play for him.

Shortly after her return home, Mrs. Maitland called the garage again by phone.

"Mrs. Faulkner phoned. She's missed a package, and believes she may have left it in the car. If you can find it, take it to her at once. . . . "

Don searched the rear seat of the Chrysler, and discovered a small package. It had slipped down between the cushions, almost out of sight.

The next moment, he had backed the car out of the garage, and was on his way to the Faulkner residence.

A pert young maid answered his ring at the door.

"A package," he said, offering it to her. "Mrs. Faulkner left it in Mrs. Maitland's car. Mrs. Maitland requested me to deliver it."

The maid grinned naughtily. "Oh, thank you, sir!" she caroled. "Madam told me to bring you right up. She wants you to deliver the package *in person!"*

Don caught the emphasis placed upon the last two words, and reddened uncomfortably. "Okay!" he said shortly, and followed the girl into the house.

Her high heels clicked like castenets. Her silk-stockinged calves flashed and shimmered. Her girlish hips swung and swayed, saucily, teasingly. She seemed to be exerting herself for Don's special pleasure.

At the door of a room on the second floor, she paused and rapped lightly. "Mrs. Maitland's chauffeur with the package," she announced.

Sounds of sudden stir inside the room. The door opened a few inches, and Mrs. Faulkner stuck her head out.

"That will be all, Marie!" she said pointedly. Then, to Don, as the maid departed: "Come right in, please! I'm dressing, but—never mind!"

Don stepped into a luxurious boudoir redolent with feminine fragrance and atmosphere of intimacy. He heard the door close firmly behind him.

As he turned, he saw with surprise that the lady was in negligee—a long, lacy garment caught carelessly together around the waist, but left to flare open both above and below. It's trailing hem swept the floor behind her.

"I wish to reward you for bringing the package," she said, with a seductive smile.

"Thank you, Ma'am," he replied. "But it isn't necessary. I was only following Mrs. Maitland's instructions, and she won't permit me to accept tips."

She laughed lightly. "I understand," she murmured. "But—let me give you a little drink!"

As she turned to cross the floor, the loose hem of her negligee trailed out in her wake, revealing feet encased in boudoir slippers, and beautiful legs bare almost to the hips. Light penetrating the lacy garment at the waist disclosed the fact that her seductive hips were covered by fancy panties, lace-trimmed and form-fitting.

Don was deeply impressed by the beauty of her figure, thrilled by sight of her feminine flesh. He absorbed the details of her appearance with appreciative eyes.

From a drawer of her dressing table, she took a bottle and a paper cup, beckoning Don closer with a motion of her head.

"Like the seasoned, old toper I am, I always have something within reach," she chuckled, tipping the neck of the bottle over the paper cup.

"Good idea!" Don murmured absently.

He was in no mood for conversation. The lady was leaning slightly forward over the dressing table, permitting Don a side view. Her negligee had gaped open, disclosing to his chocked eyes the full, firm mounds of her outjutting breasts!

Magnificent they were! Creamy white, with skin as smooth as satin. Her leaning posture caused them to droop slightly, like the unopened buds of voluptuous flowers.

"Your drink!" she said suddenly.

Don jerked himself together, and found her staring straight into his eyes, an understanding light in her own, a mocking smile on her lips.

"Er—of course!" he stammered in red-faced confusion.

His fingers trembled as he took the cup from her. But he was glad to get the drink; he needed it! He had himself under better control when he returned the cup, empty!

"You are very kind!" he said gratefully.

"Really?" Mrs. Faulkner slouched closer to him. "You've little idea how kind I *can* be, given the right opportunity—and the right man!" Her bosom rose and fell; passion smouldered in her eyes.

Don felt giddy, and his blood was on fire. The potent liquor, plus the woman's allure, was already doing things to him. He found it difficult to meet her steady gaze and retain his self-possession. Her physical charms were as powerful magnets, attracting his hands and arms!

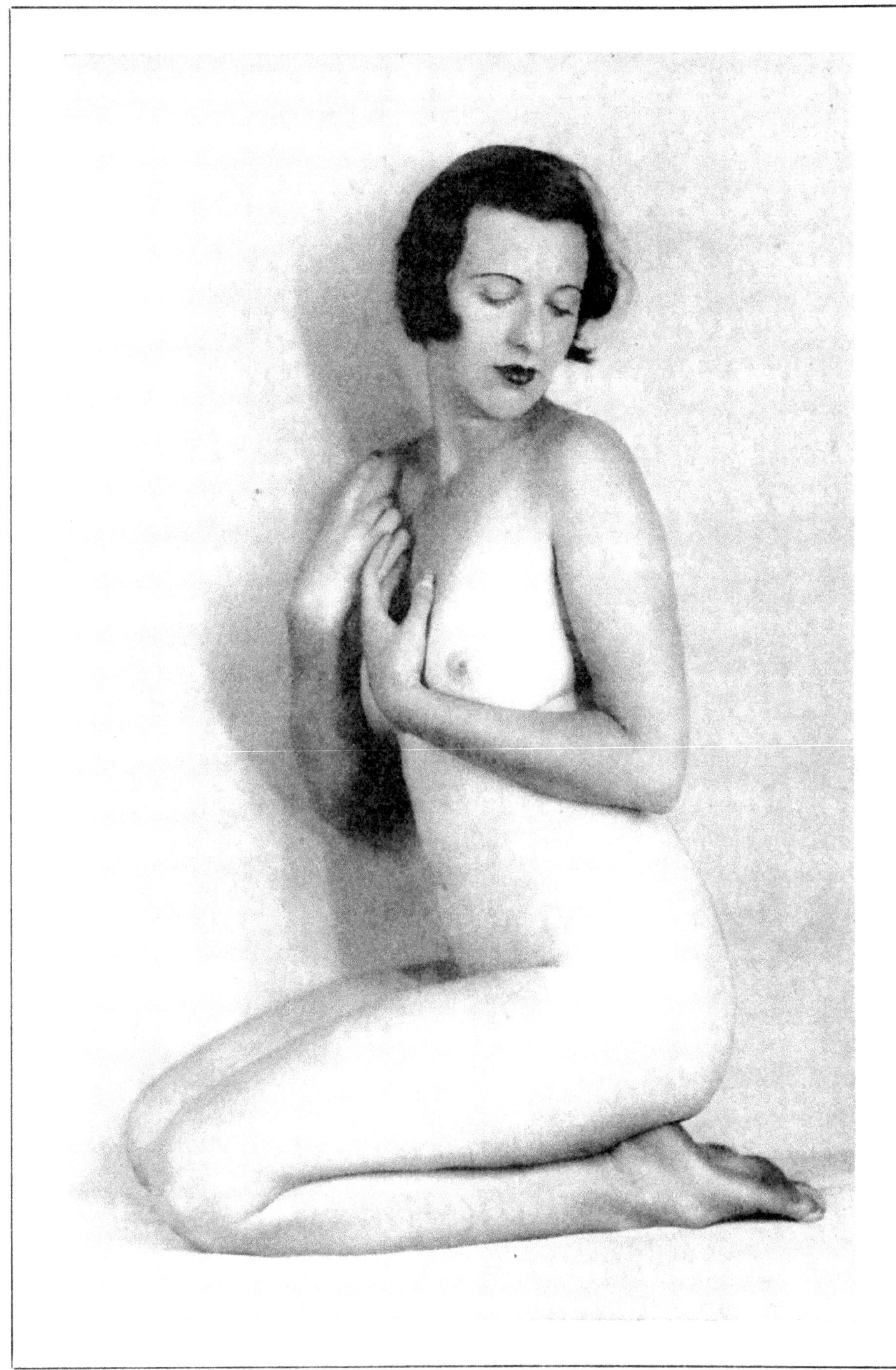

Manassé

"Er—maybe I'd better be getting back," he stammered.

"I understand—Mrs. Maitland may want you!" Mrs. Faulkner purred, following him slowly to the door. "But, surely, there are certain afternoons or evenings when you aren't engaged!"

"Oh, yes, of course."

Raising one arm, she grasped the edge of the door and leaned against it, slouching carelessly, undulating her hips so that one drooped and the other rose prominently, its voluptuous curve broad and conspicuous. Again the flaring opening at the top of the negligee revealed her proud and arrogant beauties.

"Umm!" she murmured, imitating Mae West's throaty drawl to perfection, "you must come up'n see me some time!"

Don grinned, his pulses throbbing like trip hammers. "Thanks!" he promised. "I will!"

Then, forcing his feet to do their duty, he turned and descended the stairs.

The pert young maid came forward to conduct him to the door.

"Well, did you get your reward?" she giggled saucily.

Don flushed and scowled. "For two cents," he growled menacingly, "I'd spank you!"

The maid clapped a hand over her mouth to stifle hilarious laughter and hastily closed the door.

In the afternoon, Don was called to the phone again and instructed to bring the car around to the side entrance.

When he arrived, Mrs. Maitland was already waiting for him.

She had changed from the expensive street dress to a simple, afternoon frock, a light, cool garment fashioned essentially for summer weather. She was bareheaded, and her luxurious, brown hair was lightly ruffled by the breeze.

"It's such a lovely day, I'd like to drive out into the country," she said.

"Any particular direction, Ma'am?"

"No! Just out where there are green trees and shady lanes, and quiet. Where we're not likely to meet other cars or—people!"

Don assisted her into the rear seat, observing again how well her thin dress moulded the curves of her hips and thighs; then leaped in behind the wheel, and headed the car toward the country.

His soul was singing a joyous song, for he was almost positive that Mrs. Maitland had chosen this route with deliberate design. She wished to get him alone a few minutes, to discover if he were interested in her as a woman!

Few words passed between them during the long drive through town; but an occasional glance into the mirror revealed that she had fallen into a dreamy reverie. Her dark eyes were glowing with soft lights; her cheeks were suffused with pink. Don fancied he could see the tremulous rise and fall of her bosom, as it was stirred by her excited breathing.

He chuckled to himself. Mrs. Maitland might be a novice at hooking her personal chauffeur, but at least, she was getting herself into the right mood! . . .

Presently, the car came to an intersection. The road running at right angles was a narrow lane-like affair extending deep into a wood. Little more than worn wheel tracks, it was bordered on both sides by dense shrubs and trees.

Mrs. Maitland leaned forward. "Drive down this road, Don," she instructed. "I want to see if there are any wild ferns growing in the woods."

Obediently, he turned from the main highway, chuckling to himself as he thought that there probably wasn't a house within a radius of five miles.

When the car had progressed perhaps half a mile into the woods, Mrs. Maitland suggested that he turn to one side of the road and stop.

He did so, leaving the car so surrounded by bushes that it was almost entirely concealed. Leaping down, he opened the door and helped the lady alight.

"Do you suppose we can get into the woods?" she asked breathlessly. "Wild ferns are just what I need for my window box."

"Certainly, Ma'am," he replied, grinning. "But—we'll have to climb a fence!"

"Oh, well"—in tones of affected carelessness—"I can manage."

Together they threaded a path through the bushes to the fence. Mrs. Maitland hitched up her dress and placed a slippered foot upon the lowermost rail, then paused dubiously.

"I'd better help you, Ma'am," Don murmured.

Stepping close, he slipped an arm under her warm, well-fleshed thighs, the other under her shoulders, and swung her off her feet.

"Oh!" she exclaimed faintly, grasping his shoulders with both hands. "How strong you are!"

Don merely smiled as he swung her legs over the fence and deposited her upon the topmost rail. Vaulting cleanly over, he turned with open arms to receive her.

As SHE SLIPPED into his embrace, her arms crept about his neck, and her cheek nestled warmly against his face.

"Don't put me down!" she breathed. "Hold me like this, forever!"

"I'm not strong enough to hold you that long," he laughed, clasping her passionately. "But it isn't as though I wouldn't want to!"

She nestled her seductive curves closer in his embrace, pressing against him.

For a moment they gazed, soul to soul, while waves of pink suffused her cheeks, and his heart thumped violently. The meaning in her glowing eyes was unmistakable; their gentle coaxing could not be denied.

Turning abruptly, Don carried her to a clear spot among the trees, and sank down with her upon a grassy carpet at the foot of a giant, moss-grown tree.

His crossed legs formed a cradle for her, his locked arms a hammock in which her shoulders reclined. Her arms were still raised, her hands clasped at the back of his neck. Now she drew him slowly forward, until his lips were but a scant inch from her own.

"Society frowns upon ladies who have affairs with chauffeurs," she murmured smilingly. "But, were we to be discovered now, nobody would guess that you were my chauffeur! Now, perhaps, you understand why I didn't want you to wear livery!"

"I understand," he breathed.

"And do you feel that you can grant my personal whims now and then, as well as attend to your regular duties?"

"Even better!" he assured her.

"Kiss me!"

Her lips formed the words, though no sound issued from them. Her eyes closed; she relaxed abandonedly, expectantly.

With sudden, swift fervor, Don clamped his mouth over hers, and strained her passionately to his chest. She moved slightly, and her fingernails bit into the back of his neck. Don felt hot blood surge into his temples, and his pulses throbbed like drums.

There was a long, breathless moment of delirious thoughts and ecstatic emotions. Then, gradually, he released the pressure and raised his head.

She gasped for breath, and her bosom heaved. Her eyes were starry, her lips like crushed cherries.

"Oh, Don!" she panted.

His arm slipped farther about her; his widespread fingers caressing one pulsating mound.

"But my husband must never discover!" she breathed.

"Of course not!" he assured her. He nestled his face deep in the valley of her bosom.

Even the songs of the birds were hushed by the tumult of their pounding hearts. . . .

ALMOST AN HOUR LATER, they returned to the car.

"Your ferns!" said Don, suddenly remembering. "We haven't looked for them yet!"

"Don't be silly!" chided Mrs. Maitland. "Do you think I would concern myself over a few wild weeds, when I employ a gardener to do such things for me? . . . "

A MOMENT ALONE

THE TRIM HULL of the *Shelmerdene* gleamed whitely against the inky blackness of the Sound as the yacht moved silently and swiftly along under a blanket of a million myriad stars. Only the sparkle of laughter, the gaiety of rhythmic music and the tinkle of ice in tall cool glasses marred the stillness of the night. That was almost more than enough, Noel Marsdon reflected, as he surveyed his guests from a vantage point at the rail astern. Tall, tanned to a deep bronze from months of sun along the Cote d'Azure, Noel's gaze was deeply sardonic tonight.

Why had he come? Rather, why had he had all these people come? He smiled cynically; at least, having thirty women aboard was better than one alone. There was safety in numbers.

The steward touched his arm deferentially: "The lady in Cabin Three wishes to see you, sir."

"Lady?" Noel's voice was mocking. "I'm busy; tell her I can't come," he added curtly to the steward.

"It was said to be very urgent, sir."

Noel frowned. "Oh, all right. Damn it, doesn't a man ever have a moment alone?" It was strange for him to feel that way. No one else was responsible for the party. With

By
RICHARD B.
ESPEY

"Noel!" she cried. "I couldn't help it! I didn't know what to do with her!"

the closing of the show that night, he'd invited the entire cast of "Step Ashore, Sailor!" for a midnight cruise.

He made his way slowly to Cabin Three and knocked on the door. There was no answer. Trying the knob, Noel pushed open the door and stepped inside the semi-darkness of the cabin.

"Who—who is it?" a perturbed feminine voice called jerkily.

"Me. Why?" Noel found the light switch and snapped it on, only to draw back suddenly.

Sitting on the bed before him was a lissome, dark eyed brunette, partially disrobed. That is to say, she had removed her dress to reveal a delectable figure clothed in but the minimum of lingerie, a tight fitting one piece garment clinging intimately to the luscious roundness of her breasts.

Though Noel was far from unappreciative of feminine beauty, the tone of his voice was tinged with disgust. "I might have known!" he scoffed. "Urgent business, eh? Well, I think I've heard that before, too. Why did you call for me?"

No hint of cupidity lurked in the girl's frank eyes; nor did she make any attempt to cover her scantily clad charms. "I didn't send for you," she said slowly. "I never sent for a man in my life."

"Then why are you here?" Noel demanded quizzically. "And why are you—like that? You're not bad, I must admit," he added with some slight sarcasm.

She sighed and pointed to an open porthole window where a dress on a hanger was swinging in the breeze. "Some idiot poured his cocktail on my gown," she explained. "I simply stepped in here to wait until it dried. Satisfied?" There was an edge to that last; an edge that intrigued Noel. Few women talked that way to him.

"I'm sorry," he murmured sincerely. "No doubt someone's been playing practical jokes."

She nodded and bent over to pull on her shoes. Doing so, a strap slipped from her shoulders and the one garment she wore fell away enough to reveal to Noel's eyes the tempting sight of her exquisite coral tipped bosom. Apparently unmindful of this, she arose and went to get her gown, the sheer white flesh of her unclad thighs quivering gently as she walked. One a bit less jaded than Noel would have instantly flamed to a passion inspired by the smooth velvety whiteness of her skin gleaming through the diaphanous lingerie and by the superbly molded contours of a voluptuous and almost nude figure.

Noel could not help but be amused. "For a woman with such frigid eyes," he remarked humorously, "you seem pretty casual about this business of being undressed."

The gown slipped over her shoulders, clung for an instant to her slender hips then dropped to full length as she turned about: "A girl gets used to that in the theatre," she replied. "I'm sorry you were sent on a wild goose chase on my account. It was a joke. The girls are always doing that to someone like me. They probably knew I had my clothes off and they wanted to see if I could intrigue you offstage as well as on."

She started for the door but Noel barred the way: "You do," he said levelly. "Let me talk to you."

"The answer is no," she replied coolly.

"Do you know who I am?" Noel persisted.

"No—and the answer is still no! There's only one proposition that interests me; and men of your kind rarely invest in wedding rings."

"Your show closed tonight, didn't it?" Noel demanded. She nodded and he continued, "You won't be able to get another booking right away and I've got a job that'll pay you well. How would you like to read in the morning papers tomorrow that Noel Marsdon and—whoever you are—eloped after a midnight yachting party and were married by a Gretna Green justice of the peace?"

"You're drunk!" the girl flared at him.

"Never more sober."

"Then you're crazy! You wouldn't want to marry me."

"Who said anything about getting married? I want a woman who'll live in my apartment and pose as my wife for as long as I desire. If you'd ever been what they call a playboy, you'd understand. I want to be free from the hot headed women who hang on like leeches. If people think I'm married, it'll help a lot."

"But the justice of the peace, the elopement—?" the girl echoed weakly.

"All faked; just like the marriage. Don't get me wrong; I want a wife in name only. There'll be no monkey business. Are you game?"

"I—I'll think it over," she murmured faintly.

"Good! We'll be back in New York at about three. If you're willing, slip into my car. I'll meet you there."

"Wait a minute," she demanded, "what made you pick on me?"

Noel smiled pleasantly. "Because you're the only woman on board who had a chance to pull some funny stuff—and didn't! Please understand that I'm quite normal; but I like to do my own hunting in this game they call love. Now, shall we rejoin the party? If they see us coming up from below, it'll make the news of our elopement all the more convincing."

Convincing or not, it staggered Park Avenue and those of Broadway who knew Gay Briarly to find that she and Noel Marsdon had gotten themselves married during the wee small hours of the night. The papers said in "Connecticut," but all that had happened was that Noel had driven Gay directly to his apartment where she had gone to her room and he to his.

"A swell arrangement, I think," Noel advanced as they breakfasted together and read the varied accounts of their leap into matrimony. "I just told them we'd gone across the state line; I didn't mention the exact place for fear they might check up."

He flattered himself to think that he'd been

able to pick up such an attractive bride on very short notice; for Gay was really quite charming in her pretty negligee. Her eyes met Noel's and she smiled faintly. "How am I supposed to pass the time as Mrs. Marsdon—in name only?" she inquired.

Noel peeled off several bills and handed them to her. "Lots of women can find something to do if they've got that. There's more whenever you need it. All I ask is that you come home nights, just to make it look real! You probably won't see much of me; I feel freer than I have for years, and I want to make the most of my freedom. I suppose that's hard to understand."

"No," Gay replied, "but what makes you think you'll have more freedom if people think you're married?"

"Listen!" he leaned across the table towards her, "when I pick 'em they're good! Anybody'd be a fool to think that I'd run out on a wife as good looking as you are. A few touches by Saks *et al* and you'll be Park Avenue's number one lady!"

When Noel dropped in again that afternoon, he found that he hadn't spoken out of turn. Gay was attractive to begin with; and garbed in the newest and most chic manner she was enchanting. Noel glanced at her with approval.

"You like it?" Gay asked eagerly.

"It's wonderful!" Then, lest he seem too appreciative, added, "I like to see any woman dress well. I shan't be here for dinner," he informed her. "In fact, you probably won't see much of me at all! This plan has worked like a charm; it's thrown off almost all of those females whom I wanted to shake and left me free to go after the others."

"Then there are others? I mean women whom you want to go after, as you say."

Noel shot her a quizzical glance. "I've never had a chance to chase a woman. It's always been the other way around. Oh, don't

"I never sent for a man in my life!" she explained.

think I'm conceited. If I were poor, I shouldn't be troubled at all," he added wryly, departing for his room to change to evening clothes.

For several days Noel was constantly on the wing, hitting all of Manhattan's motley array of high spots and playing no favorites. If anyone cared to lift an eyebrow to the fact that he wasn't seen very much with his wife, Noel let them lift it; but Broadway being the street it is, few did.

As for Gay, she managed to pass the time doing a little bit of everything. Having nothing to do and quite a lot of money to do it with doesn't pall on one immediately. It was perhaps the third day of her "marriage" when she decided to spend an afternoon doing nothing at all, except reading and enjoying a discreet cocktail.

Some hours had passed pleasantly in this manner when she heard the door to the apartment softly opening. Without turning around or rising from her chair, she called out, "That you, Noel?"

It was a distinct surprise to hear a husky feminine voice in a deep throated reply, "No, my dear. Were you expecting him?"

Gay arose quickly and faced her caller, a tall sinuous blonde with glittering icy eyes. "Who are you?" she asked, not impolitely.

THE BLONDE CASUALLY tossed her wrap into a chair and sat down in another to light a cigarette: "Rea Drake," she supplied briefly. "Now who are you?"

"Why—why, don't you know?" Gay asked hesitantly.

Rea Drake smiled insolently: "It was in the papers, wasn't it? But I read between the lines. Something tells me that you're nothing but a dumb little chorine who was lucky enough to pull a fast one on Noel. Cheap tricks to cheap women!"

Gay flushed crimson, "How dare you!" she flared angrily. "I'd like to know what right you have to come breaking in here like this?"

"The right any women has to claim the man she loves. Your kind doesn't know the meaning of love. A marriage ceremony - - bah! You probably got him tight and tricked him into believing he'd married you when he came to. I've been to Gretna Green, Stamford and Greenwich - - - There hasn't been a marriage license issued to Noel Marsdon in any of those places!"

"And what do you propose to do?" Gay shot back at her.

"Noel loves me, and I'll show you how a woman gets the man she loves—without tricks!" Turning on her heel, she went rapidly toward Noel's bedroom. "A woman who's really attractive has but to make her man conscious of that!" she flung back over her shoulder.

Gay followed her into the bedroom only to gasp in dismay as she perceived what Rea Drake's intentions were. Speechless, Gay saw her hastily beginning to discard her clothes. Her gown dropped to the floor and she stood before Gay, audaciously revealed in the sheerest of lingerie. Two saucy kicks and her shoes had joined the dress.

"You're not going to—" Gay murmured, horrified and at a total loss for knowledge of what to do.

"But I am!" the blonde flipped recklessly as she peeled off her hosiery. Brazenly she slipped down the shoulder straps of her chemise and turned about to taunt Gay. "You see, my dear; a man does not have to be intoxicated to appreciate my charms!" Her hands lovingly caressed her unconfined breasts as she pirouetted before the mirror, quite nude but for the chemise that clung to her svelte hips. Another instant and this too was gone. Completely unclad, she smiled brazenly. "You'd better run along! When Noel comes, send him to me!"

Gay was far from being a prude but as she left the blonde alone, she was too amazed to be able to think clearly. The clicking latch of the door only served to throw her into a panic.

"Noel!" she cried desperately as he entered. "I—I couldn't help it! I didn't know what to do! She's in there!"

"Who's in there?" he demanded frowning.

"Rea Drake. And Noel, she's taken off her clothes! She's going to stay!"

His lips formed to a half smile, "Going to stay, eh? How nice!" With brisk strides he crossed the room, entered the bedroom and closed the door after him while Gay sank dizzily into a chair. Would Rea's daring have the desired effect? Gay had to admit that she was attractive, alluring to the nth degree. Would Noel——?

"Get out!" His brusque command put an end to her questions. The door had been flung open and through it Gay saw Rea getting back into her clothes with almost as much speed as she had shown in discarding them. Noel stood in the doorway, his eyes flashing fire.

In a minute Rea emerged and glared at Gay, "You lied to him!" she flamed hotly. "If it hadn't been for you—"

"Out!" Noel's clipped precise tone brooked no further delay. He held open the door to the apartment, waited while Rea stomped imperiously out, then closed it and returned to Gay. "Sorry," he murmured apologetically. "Rea is sometimes a bit forward."

"Isn't that putting it rather mild?" Gay smiled.

"I hope it didn't upset you."

"Not me, but how about you? To come home and find a woman in one's room, undressed, would seem a bit distracting."

"There are thousands of them. But let's change the subject. If you don't have any other plans, I thought we might spend a quiet evening at home. You know, a nice dinner, a little radio music and maybe a bit of backgammon. Would domesticity pall on you for one evening?"

"Oh, no," Gay answered quickly. "I'd like it; only I don't know much about backgammon!"

"You can learn! I'll phone down to the restaurant now and have them send something up. You might try your luck with a few cocktails."

NOEL HAD SUGGESTED this sort of an evening merely on an impulse of the moment. As they dined together, he was surprised that it was turning out so enjoyably. Very peaceful and very restful—qualities that he had sought but rarely. Gay told him much of a side of the theater that Noel hadn't seen; of her experiences as a trouper in vaudeville, one night stands and carnivals.

"Men?" she smiled in response to his query. "Don't you see that I haven't had much time, nor even a chance to meet the sort of men who might really appeal to a girl?"

At that moment, there was a loud knock on the door. Noel answered it and started in amazement as a fat, stodgy man of about forty burst into the room. Without a word he pointed an accusing finger at Gay and muttered angrily.

"At last I've got you! And you're not gonna get away this time!"

"Do you know him?" Noel questioned.

"Never saw him in my life."

"Hah!" the man exclaimed. "That's good! Listen you," he turned to Noel, "I married this dame two years ago in Tulsa. Now she claims she's married to you! Looks damn funny to me."

"It's not true!" Gay cried out. "He's lying!"

"Got a rich papa now, eh, honey?" the man leered. "Well, I don't mind, but it's gonna cost him something to square it with me."

Noel's reply to that was a stiff right to the intruder's jaw that sent him reeling to the hallway. Closing the door, he shot Gay an inquiring glance. "Blackmail, eh? If the two of you are in on this, I've been a sucker for fair!"

Gay burst into tears and rushed to her room while Noel slumped dismally into a chair. Women and trouble always went together, especially if a man happened to have cash in the bank. He drew out his checkbook and began to calculate just how much he'd have to pay her. After a moment or so, he arose and started for her bedroom.

The telephone's ring halted him; and when he finally entered Gay's room he was smiling strangely, rather than frowning.

What was his surprise to find Gay angrily discarding her finery and ransacking the closet for her own less expensive and less smart clothes.

"Oh, Gay!" Noel called softly.

She faced him unhappily, her eyes dimmed with tears. Her only attire consisted of two brief pieces of lingerie. "I'm giving them back!" she uttered morosely. "Everything! You might as well have these, too, I suppose!" And before Noel could say anything, she began unhooking the brassiere before his entranced gaze.

"Gay!" Noel whispered fervently, and stepped toward her suddenly to take her in his arms. "I—I love you! I admit I thought it was a blackmail racket until just now. Rea phoned me to ask if I'd heard about your husband—and I smelled a rat. It's just the kind of a trick she'd play—but she phoned too soon!"

"You mean you want me to stay—?" Gay murmured softly, her vibrant and lithe figure molded to his.

"Forever and forever!" Noel answered as his hands began a delightful caress that explored hitherto unheard of pleasures. "And this time, we'll make it real! A license and everything!"

"First you might kiss me! And after that, well, we were going to play backgammon tonight. Remember?"

"Backgammon?" Noel echoed, sweeping her gorgeous body into his embrace. "If one's in love, backgammon's quite unnecessary!"

And so it seemed that night!

When In Rome....

By

TOM KANE

JUDGED by ordinary standards, Judy Barbour was not a raving beauty. She was not even pretty in the chorus girl fashion. It was the irregularity of her features that kept her out of the beauty class, and it was in the unusualness of her personality that the difference lay between her and the average chorus girl.

She was not very tall, and she was very slender. Her hair was thick, almost black, and usually in a state of wild confusion. Her dark eyes had a tendency to slant, and at times she looked as if there was more than just a dash of the oriental in her. She had a straight, aquiline nose, and a full, sensuous mouth. Her teeth were large, even and very white. There was an intensity about her which was at once arresting and not a little frightening. One either liked Judy or one hated her.

Her body was beautiful, and she handled it gracefully. Her breasts were small, round and placed high upon her. She had a narrow waist, wide hips and long, tapering legs. Her hands and feet were small, and her arms delicately rounded and soft. When she spoke, her enunciation was perfect, and her voice low and vibrant.

Mrs. Arthur Trout watched her musingly as she sat before the mirror, making up her face. Over a pair of scanty panties, she had tossed a flowing kimono, and Mrs. Trout watched the graceful movement of her bare arms with pride and affection.

After a while, Mrs. Trout said, "Dear, I don't want to rub it in, but I suppose you realize that this is about our last chance?"

"I suppose so," answered Judy wearily. "How I hate this social system! I see very little difference between our so-called democracy and the sternest monarchy that ever existed."

"The only difference is," Mrs. Trout agreed, "that our social system is based on money, whereas the other's based on caste. But it amounts to the same thing in the long run." She sighed. "Too bad, Judy; but it can't be helped."

Judy continued listlessly with her make-up. "Sometimes," she said, "I wish I'd been born a salesgirl, or a waitress or something like that. At least I'd be able to choose my own life."

"Well, you weren't, Judy, and that's all there is to it. You may as well make up your mind to the fact that we're absolutely broke, that there isn't the faintest hope of any more money coming in, and that the only hope for us lies in a wealthy marriage for you."

Judy muttered something nasty under her breath.

Mrs. Trout shrugged her plump shoulders. "It can't be helped," she said. "You can't beat the system. Have you ever met Ronnie Savage?"

"No. Have you?"

"Yes, some time ago. He's young, he's handsome and he's very charming. I don't think, Judy, you'd find being married to him such a difficult task. And he has millions, with more millions in the offing."

Judy commenced to brush her hair briskly. "Damn, damn, damn!" she said feelingly.

Mrs. Trout smiled sympathetically, rose and went over to her. She sat down on half the bench. She said, "You're not in love with Stew, are you, Judy?"

Judy shook her head. "No. That's all over long ago. I like Stew, I like him a lot, but I've been out of love with him for a long time."

"Does he know it?"

"Yes, but he still has hopes. He got us invited here because he thought the lake, the moon, the romance and all the rest of it, would make me susceptible."

"Did he know that Ronnie Savage was going to be here, too?"

"I don't know." She smiled bitterly. "Even if he did, I don't suppose it would've occurred to him that I was going to throw myself at Ronnie's head."

"Stew's a nice boy, Judy, but he's not of the same caste, and he doesn't understand the system." Suddenly Mrs. Trout's eyes narrowed, and a metallic note entered her voice as she continued. "Judy," she said, "you must allow nothing to interfere with your plans.

Stoop to anything, but . . . get that man! It's absolutely our one and only hope. Can I depend on you?"

Judy looked at her aunt's set face and smiled. She patted one of her hands. "Don't worry about it, Auntie," she said. "When in Rome, and all the rest of it. I'm part of the system, and much as I hate it . . . I'll do my part."

"That's a good girl, Judy. I always knew I could depend on you."

THEY WERE DANCING on the terrace under a canopy of Japanese lanterns. The cloudless sky was bright with stars, and there was a slight tang to the early autumn air. The strains of the orchestra were sweet and soft, and a gigantic table at the far end of the terrace had been turned into a well-stocked bar. Judy was in the arms of Stew, her body was against his, and his lips were against her hair.

Stew was saying, "It's hell loving someone

"Our only hope lies in a wealthy marriage for you," said her Aunt.

as much as I love you, Judy, knowing that you don't love me."

"I'm sorry, Stew. It just isn't there any more. I wish it were, but it isn't."

"Is there someone else?"

"No." They danced for some little time in silence, then as casually as she could Judy said, "Which is Ronnie Savage?"

"Haven't you met Ronnie?"

"No."

Stew looked about him at the swirling dancers. Presently he indicated a couple swaying slowly on the outskirts of the floor. Judy looked. Ronnie was almost as dark as she was. He was very tall and well-built. He looked splendid in well-cut evening clothes, and Judy noticed that he was a superb dancer.

His companion was a tall blonde. Beautiful, sophisticated-looking, and obviously not a woman to be trifled with.

Judy said, "Who's the girl he's with?"

"Rita Wilde. She's been trying to land Ronnie for the last two years, but he isn't having any."

"Doesn't want to marry, eh?"

"Ronnie's scared of marriage. He always feels that it's his money the women are after. He's a nice chap. Like to meet him?"

"Yes. He's a beautiful dancer, isn't he?"

"Not bad."

The saxophone announced that there was to be a brief respite, and the dancers clustered about the bar. Taking Judy by the elbow, Stew led her over, and pushed and shoved until he was alongside Ronnie and the blonde. They turned to him.

"Aye-there, Stew—how they coming?"

"Swell, Ronnie. Aye-there, Rita. Judy, this is Rita Wilde—Judy Barbour." The girls nodded, and for a fraction of a second their eyes met. They distrusted each other instantly. "Ronnie, Judy . . . Judy, Ronnie." They smiled and shook hands.

"What'll you have?" said Ronnie to Judy.

"What is there?"

"Just about everything. How about a champagne cocktail?"

"Nice."

"Oke. Stew, fix Rita up, will you?" The two women edged closer to the bar, and Judy and Rita stared at each other.

"Strange we've never met before," said Rita. "We seem to move in the same circles."

"I've spent a lot of my time in England and on the Continent."

"Really? Nice having you here tonight." She smiled with her lips only. The men returned and handed the girls their drinks. Ronnie instantly attached himself to Judy.

"Before we go any further," he said, "may I have the next dance?"

"With a great deal of pleasure," answered Judy. Her dark eyes were upon him, and Ronnie blinked. Then he grinned.

"Here's how!" They drank slowly. Stew and Rita had drifted away, and already the crowd was beginning to thin. The orchestra commenced to play, and Ronnie took the two glasses and handed them to a passing waiter. "Come along," he said, and slipped his arm about Judy's waist.

They danced beautifully together. Ronnie held her close against him. His hand rested lightly in the middle of her naked back, and the pressure of her arm about his neck was perhaps a little stronger than was absolutely necessary.

"You have a lovely figure," said Ronnie.

Judy gazed up at him and smiled. The light glistened on her teeth and danced in her dark eyes. "I'm glad you like it," she said.

"Are you always as generous with it as you're being to me?"

Judy shook her head. "No. I'm very particular."

"Then you must like me."

Judy came just a little closer, and her voice was husky as she said, "I do like you."

They were in a dark corner, and before Judy realized what had happened, Ronnie was kissing her passionately. His arms hurt her, and his lips was jammed against hers. Judy felt the blood racing through her veins, and she went limp in his arms. Then the music ceased, they released each other and stood apart. Before they could say anything, Rita joined them.

Imperiously, she said, "Please buy me a drink, Ronnie."

RONNIE GATHERED HIMSELF together with a visible effort, slipped his arm through both girls' arms and led them over to the bar. He ordered the drinks, and as the bartender turned away he glanced at Judy, who winked back at him. When the bartender handed Rita her drink, Judy's eyes narrowed as she watched Rita raise the glass to her lips. They drank slowly, then Rita dragged Ronnie away. Over his shoulder, excitedly, Ronnie said,

"See you later, Judy!"

Judy nodded vaguely, watched them disappear through the crowd, then followed them. Presently she heard their voices from the other side of a tall hedge. Deliberately, she listened.

She heard Rita say languidly, "Let's get away from here, Ronnie. It's hot and there're too many people about."

"Where shall we go?"

"Let's take one of the canoes and go places."

"Okay. You go and get a wrap or something, and I'll meet you down at the landing-stage."

"Yes, Ronnie. Kiss me."

Judy listened to the silence that followed, and instinctively her hands wandered over her breasts. She wished it were she who was with Ronnie instead of Rita. So far Ronnie had made little actual impression on her, but she liked him well enough, and she was determined that she was going to continue with her plan to marry him if possible. She went back onto the terrace, and from a shadowed corner watched Rita as she proceeded through the crowd to get her wrap. She loked all right, but Judy knew the bartender of old. He could spike a drink along with the best of them. It wouldn't be long now for Rita.

Judy waited a bit, then went to the dressing room. As she expected, Rita was stretched out on a couch, fast asleep. That last drink certainly was a strong one. Judy smiled, threw a shawl about her shoulders and left the long, rambling old house.

then a voice. Ronnie's voice. He said, "That you, Rita?"

Judy walked to the edge of the jetty and looked over. Ronnie, balancing a paddle across his knees, sat in a small canoe, some ten feet below her.

"We'll break into that large bungalow on the island!" he yelled.

Quickly, she made her way through the silent grounds. The moon winked at her through the overhanging branches, and she was anything but happy. She did not like her life particularly. The lake came into view, and presently the short wooden jetty leading out into it. Nonchalantly, her shawl clutched about her, Judy walked out on the jetty. From below, came a soft whistle, and

She said, "Sorry, no. What're you doing there?"

Ronnie grinned up at her in the moonlight. "I was waiting for Rita," he answered frankly.

Judy laughed softly. "You'll have a long wait, then," she told him. "I just saw her in the middle of a stiff necking party with Stew. And if I know my Stew, it'll be some little time before he unscrambles himself."

Ronnie's face clouded, and he watched her as she leaned against a small bollard.

Ronnie said, "How about coming for a cruise with me?"

"What about Rita?"

"To hell with Rita! Like to come?"

Judy gazed up at the moon. "I don't know," she said at last.

"Come on. Nice and cool down here."

"You wouldn't take advantage of a girl?"

Ronnie grinned. "That'ud be rather difficult in a canoe, wouldn't it?"

"I suppose it would, really. All right." Judy pulled her shawl about her and went slowly down the weedy ladder. Ronnie held the frail craft steady while she stepped gingerly into it, then cast off and dipped his paddle.

"Where shall we go?" he asked.

Judy sighed and trailed her slender hand in the water. "Anywhere," she said dreamily.

Ronnie paddled on in silence, the water dripping from the blade like jewels in the white moonlight. Judy commenced to move about, leaning over the side and reaching into the water. Ronnie said, "Take it easy. This isn't the *Majestic,* you know. It doesn't take much to upset one of these."

"I want to catch a fish," said July. She leaned still farther over the side, and the canoe tipped alarmingly.

"Hey!" said Ronnie. The next thing they knew they were in the water, clinging to the bottom of the canoe. They came up on either side of it, and stared at each other across the top. "You little donkey," said Ronnie, grinning and wiping the water from his eyes.

"I'm sorry," said Judy. "Will we drown?"

Ronnie shook his head. "We're more liable to freeze first. There's nothing we can do. Even if we did right the canoe, we've lost the paddle and we could only drift on this hellish current.

"What'll we do?" said Judy.

"Hang on until we drift to that island. And there, little lady, I fear me we're stuck until the morning. Unless they miss us and come after us."

Judy said nothing. There was nothing for her to say. After a while, Ronnie said, "We may as well swim. It'll keep us warm in the first place, and secondly, we'll get there much quicker."

"Yes," said Judy faintly. She wished that she had not done this thing now. After a while, she said, "Is there some kind of hut or something on the island?"

"Yes. There's a large bungalow. We'll probably have to break in. There isn't anybody there now."

They swam on, pushing the canoe ahead of them. Presently, they touched bottom, and waded out of the water. Ronnie righted the canoe and carried it a little way up the beach. Shivering with the cold wind in their soaking clothes, they climbed up the beach, entered the surrounding belt of trees, and eventually arrived on the porch of a one-story log cabin. Ronnie tried to break down the door without success. Judy stood and shivered miserably while he went out to the woodshed and presently returned with an axe. Two or three lusty blows, and the door fell in. They entered, leaving a trail of water behind them. Ronnie switched on the light. They found themselves in a large living room, out of which opened a series of bedrooms. Ronnie indicated one and said,

"In there, you might find some clothes."

"Thanks." Judy left him and closed the door after her.

She stripped off her dripping gown, her sodden underwear, shoes and stockings. From a drawer in the bureau, she took a rough turkish towel and dried herself thoroughly, then she looked about for clothes. All she could find was a pair of sailor pants, some sneakers and a sweatshirt. She put them on and felt warmer. Then she went out once more into the living room. Ronnie, in much the same ill-fitting outfit, had got a fire blazing in the open fireplace, and a bottle of brandy and two glasses stood on a small table at the head of a couch facing the fire. He grinned at Judy and led her over to the couch. He pushed her into it, poured her a stiff drink, and handed it to her. They drank in silence until their glasses were empty. Then Judy lay back and stared at the fire.

In a small voice, she said, "I'm sorry, Ronnie. I didn't mean to inconvenience you."

Ronnie dropped his hand to the back of hers. "I think I'm going to like being—inconvenienced," he said softly.

Judy's eyes met and held his. "We mustn't do anything like that," she said. "As it is, I'm compromised beyond repair. Oh, dear . . . oh, dear . . . ." she dropped her head to her hands and sobbed. Doing a very good job of it. Ronnie put his arm about her shaking shoulders.

"Don't take it like that," he said softly. "They'll understand. It was an accident."

"But my mother! What on earth is she

going to think? I suppose there isn't a telephone here?" Ronnie shook his head, and Judy commenced to weep softly. Ronnie gave them both another stiff drink, and tossed more logs onto the fire. They sat there for some little time sipping their brandy and looking into the blazing logs.

After a while, putting down his empty glass, Ronnie said, "You're very beautiful, Judy. I suppose you know that?"

"I'm not really. It's just the brandy and the firelight."

"I think you're beautiful." He came closer to her and before she knew what he was doing, he had taken her in his arms, and was kissing her tenderly.

Judy lay limp in his arms. Her emotions were mixed. She did not know whether she liked it or not, and none of the elation she should have felt was there. Ronnie bent her back on the couch, and transferred his lips from hers to her hair. He kissed her hair, her large, moist eyes, her cheeks and finally her mouth again. This time, little quivers of excitement passed up and down Judy's spine, and she found herself reacting to him and her arms stole about him. Ronnie held her close, and his hands slipped beneath the sweatshirt. She could feel his fingers against the naked flesh of her back. She felt his hands slide under her arms, and then she felt him touching—ever so lightly—her round and pointed breasts, and a little sigh escaped her. Ronnie kissed her again, and his fingers sent delicious thrills and chills through her pulsating body.

"Ronnie," she whispered, "this is all wrong!"

"No, it isn't. Will you marry me, Judy?"

"But you don't love me."

"I've loved you all my life. Will you?"

"Yes. I love you."

And then Ronnie switched out the light. The current lapped against the distant beach, and all that could be heard was the sound of sighs.

Just before dawn, Judy slipped into her still damp clothes. Quietly, so as not to waken Ronnie, she stole out of the cabin and walked to the beach. She had never been so miserable in her life, and she knew she wasn't going through with it. She had fallen violiently in love with Ronnie, and she was going to tell him, should she ever see him again, how she had tricked him. She hated herself.

(*Please turn to page* 63)

"You're very beautiful, Judy! I suppose you know that."

Winding Roads

By

KAY CARROLL

THE mists of a warm summer evening were beginning to shroud the countryside. The scent of new mown hay was in the air, and the lowing of cows at milking time accentuated the bucolic atmosphere.

On a white ribbon of road, threading the Shenandoah Valley, an automobile meandered at a less accelerated though noisier pace than an ancient snail.

"Listen to the crickets and the katy-dids!" said Lucy Matthews, who was lounging beside her husband in the front seat.

"That means another hot day tomorrow!" replied Tom Matthews, keeping a firm grip on the wheel.

Lucy turned to toss the little jacket of her knitted silk-and-wool sports suit on to the rear cushions of the car, already crowded by a miscellany of bags and blankets and packages.

"If it's as hot as today I'll pass out!" she remarked, plucking at the knit blouse that limned her lushly full figure. "Did you say that an auto tour was a nice, cool way to spend a vacation?"

"Sure it is!" he laughed. "Just loping leisurely through strange country, happy-go-lucky, without a care, watching the changing scenery as the winding road unravels before you, beckoning you on and on . . . time means nothing, because tomorrow is another day!"

"Oh, yes!" Lucy's tone was sarcastic. "A day of dust and heat and perspiration, and a night of mosquitos humming and stinging so you can't sleep!"

"I think it's romantic!" retorted Tom, stubbornly.

"And I think it's a crazy idea." Lucy studied her complexion in a hand mirror. "I'm getting freckles on my nose and the wind is drying my skin to the stiffness of parchment paper!"

"You brought plenty of cold cream!" he muttered.

Lucy ignored the gibe. Her big brown eyes, flecked with onyx tints, seemed weary as she continued: "I haven't slept in a comfortable bed or had a decent bath since we left home three days ago."

"That's the fun of it, staying out in the country and keeping away from the big towns!" asserted Tom.

"It might be fun to you, but it's a pain to me." She lighted one of his cigarettes and settled back in her seat.

"I don't see why you should be so unfortunately uncomfortable riding along like this." He glanced at her. "If I remember correctly, you're wearing nothing but a smile under that pretty dress."

"Not even a smile!" she said.

It wasn't difficult to believe the truth of her statement. . . . She had crossed her knees, revealing stockings rolled below bare kneecaps and a glimpse of creamy skin at the beginning of softly contoured thighs. Her hips were etched with astonishing clarity, and the jutting roundness of her breasts had a faintly perceptible droop which added piquancy to their voluptuous prominence and gave away the secret that no brassiere was now hugging or lifting them.

Tom grasped the wheel with one hand, and laid his palm on a smooth kneecap.

"Cheer up, honey!" he said. "I'll give you a break tonight and stop at the next town. There ought to be a good hotel there, with hot water and private bathtubs and eiderdown beds and all the trimmings of home!"

"Don't kid me!" she murmured, the vehemence of her sigh distending and raising her breasts. "If I ever get into such a hotel, you'll never get me out."

"Cheerio!" grinned Tom.

"How far away it this imaginary town and mythical hotel?"

"A few miles!"

"Thank heaven!"

Lucy sighed again. . . . It looked as though the knitted silk could never stand the strain of the upward heave of that bosom!

CHUGGING DOWN THE main street of the town, the car halted in front of a four-story building which bore the single word: "Hotel".

"It doesn't look very encouraging to me!" commented Lucy. "If they have a private bath in that place, I'll eat it for supper."

Tom smiled. "You sit here and I'll go in and make arrangements!" he said. "Or would you like to come in with me?"

"Go ahead . . . I'll wait . . . I think you're too optimistic, anyway." She returned his smile, however, as pleasantly as she could under the circumstances that were irritating to her.

"It'll be the third time I've bathed in a bucket!" she said. "I'm wondering if I'll ever see a bathtub again?"

"You sarcasm doesn't help matters any!" he stated, acidly.

Lucy pinched his leg, laughing. "Forgive me, dear!" she murmured. "I know it's not your fault, but there ought to be good hotel accommodations everywhere. . . . At least, I thought so when I consented to take this trip with you. . . . But we'll make the best of things!"

"Run along and bring me that bucket of water," she ordered.

Tom wasn't absent long. . . . And when he faced Lucy again, his face was frowning.

"I'm sorry!" he said. "There isn't a vacant room left in the hotel . . . but there's a good auto tourist camp a mile out of town, so the clerk said."

Lucy laughed sardonically.

"I thought you were wasting your time!" she exclaimed, kicking the dashboard with the point of her shoe. "Come on, Tommy darling, let's be on our way to the tourist camp . . . we're tourists, anyway, aren't we?"

Tom grumpily resumed his seat behind the wheel.

"There'll be a well and a pump and we can draw a bucket of cold water for ourselves!" she went on. "That'll be lots of fun, won't it?"

He shifted gears savagely.

"That sounds more sporty!" smiled Tom.

On the outskirts of town, the car swerved off the main road, obeying a sign that pointed toward a grove of trees through which the glint of the setting sun could be seen on the waters of a tiny lake.

"Pretty spot!" said Tom.

"Lovely!" agreed Lucy.

The banks of the lake were dotted by one-room cabins, a larger one bearing the appearance of a general store, and on its *facade* was a sign: *"Bungalows to Let!"*

"We're here because we're here . . ." Lucy hummed the song, jumping out of the car. Tom had already disappeared inside the store, emerging with a key and a grin.

"Cabin No. 9" he announced.

"Show me the way to go home!" Lucy switched into another song, as she fell in with Tom's stride. He unlocked the cabin door and ushered her inside.

"Not bad!" he commented.

"Just like all the rest!" she retorted. "But where's the pump? . . . I simply must have my bucket of water, darling!"

He put his arms about her, kissing her supper." He glanced at his watch. "We'll eat in the restaurant over at the general store. . . . I've ordered fried chicken and potatoes and hot biscuits and apple pie!"

"That's a hungry man's meal!" she smiled.

"Does it suit you?" he asked.

"Perfectly, sweetheart, especially when I don't have to cook it." She kicked off her shoes. "Leave some cigarettes, will you? And

Lucy sat down on the grass. "Who — who are you?" she murmured.

moistened lips. "Are you really having such an uncomfortable trip?"

"Well, to tell the truth, I've enjoyed better vacations!" she said, returning his kiss. "But run along and bring me that bucket of water."

He soon returned with it. "There!" he said. "You'll be a real camper some of these days." His arm went around her, his fingers stirring in the softness of the breasts that had been taunting him all day.

Lucy's mouth hotly responded to the foraging of his lips, and then she playfully pushed him away. "Go on outside and listen to the birdies in the trees while I take my bucket bath."

Tom laughed. "Go to it, honey! I'm going to leave you for a while, anyway. My brakes need tightening, and I'll run the car into the town garage and have it looked over before don't be longer than you can help, because my tummy is empty and your talk of fried chicken makes it feel emptier."

"Flat as a pancake!" he murmured, passing his hand intimately. "But this isn't flat!" One palm traversed the swelling curves of her hips and the other cupped the upstanding beauty of a breast.

"Freshy!" she whispered. "You're as full of inspiration this evening as an egg is full of meat! . . . Was it the sight of that blonde we passed this afternoon that gave you the ambition?"

"Don't be silly!"

"Nice, wasn't she?"

"Oh, she was all right!"

Tom's hands were extremely busy while Lucy was questioning him. . . . She bit her

(*Please turn to page* 56)

FRENCH MODEL PHOTOS

MEN: Get a complete assortment of Real French Type Pictures, all different. Two sets (20) different Poses, Snappy Models in reclining and other poses. One set (12) different poses, young couples in passionate love scenes. Also a couple of Paris Models—the good stuff. All Clear, well made, gloss finished, quality pictures. These are all ACTUAL photographs.

Special: Some Short Stories, and over 50 small size pictures included with the above without extra charge, also a snappy illustrated booklet. All Sent Prepaid on receipt of $1.00 cash, money order or stamps.

All for $1.00

REX SALES CO.

4166 PARK AVENUE, DEPT. P. S., NEW YORK CITY

PHOTOGRAPHS Tell the Story

GENUINE PHOTOS

Set "A"—A set of 15 wonderful girl photos in very daring and tantalizing poses to show everything to the best advantage.

Set "E"—15 revealing new cartoons, 8 of which show a daring version of The Pretty Farmer's Daughter and the Traveling Salesman. Also 7 additional cartoons each of which tell a complete story in itself. Printed on gloss photo paper.

Set "G"—16 actual photos of men and women together! Very intimate. These are the kind of photos that you keep in your inside pocket and you make sure there are no holes in the pocket either.

Set "J"—A rare set of photos never offered before. 14 of the finest, clearest Hula Girl photos. One photo shows 14 girls but most of them show only one girl in the hottest, most revealing poses in the clothes as nature intended. Most of these photos actually photographed in Hawaii.

Check sets desired. $1.00 per set or if this is your first order, we will send all four sets for $2.00.

We also have a new book title "For Men Only." Spicy reading that Men will enjoy. Full library size, over 1 inch thick and weighs 1 pound. Price $1.50 if ordered alone or $1.00 if ordered with above photos. Express shipments only. Immediate service. Cash, stamps, money order.

NOVELTY STUDIO

P. O. Box 499 Rockford, Ill.

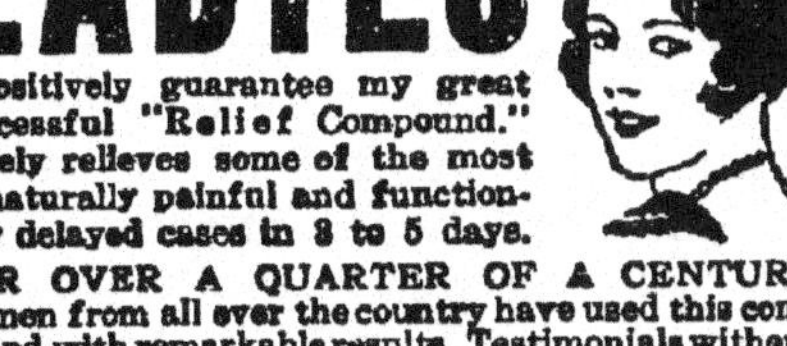

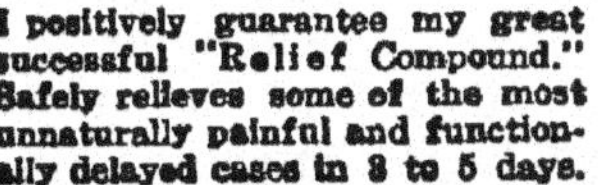

I positively guarantee my great successful "Relief Compound." Safely relieves some of the most unnaturally painful and functionally delayed cases in 3 to 5 days.

FOR OVER A QUARTER OF A CENTURY women from all over the country have used this compound with remarkable results. Testimonials without number. No harm, pain or interference with work. Mail, $2. Double strength, $3. Booklet Free. Also FREE with each order while they last 2 Books of 127 pages entitled "What Every Married Woman Should Know" by Fielding and "The Physiology of Sex Life" by Dr. Greer. Simply mail this ad and your order today for either single or double strength treatment to

DR. B.T. SOUTHINGTON REMEDY CO., KANSAS CITY, MO.

FRENCH PHOTOS RARE PICTURES

Taken From Life. Front views, rear views, side views. Show everything. Couples in intimate poses; also Group Pictures. And, are they hot! Developed in our own private photographic studios, and sold to grown-ups only. 6 prints for $1.00. 18 prints for $2.00.

RENE NOVELTY SHOP

1403 E. Forest Ave., Dept. 7, Detroit, Mich.

CURIOUS BOOKS

Privately Printed

THE LARGEST PUBLISHERS IN THE UNITED STATES of privately printed books on Oriental Love, Uncensored Exotics, Amatory Adventures and other Curious Sex Customs. Send for free Catalogs.

PANURGE PRESS, 70 Fifth Ave., New York
Please send me your illustrated brochures on curious, privately printed books.

Name .... Age ....

Address ....

City .... State ....

PS1

Free To Men "New VIGOR Tablets"

If you want to know what a REAL Medicine is like—a safe, snappy, tonic-stimulant, write for trial package my famous "Vigor Tablets" sent free, sealed ready for use. Used by men everywhere.

PIER CO.

19-A-72 Cortlandt Street, New York

(*Continued from page 54*)

lower lip, fluttered her eyelashes and whispered:

"You said your brakes were slipping! . . . You'd better get them fixed, and I'll pretend that bucket is a bath tub!"

Tom tossed a packet of cigarettes on the cabin's bed. "Okay!" he said. "And when I come back from the garage I'll draw another bucket for myself."

"Then we'll eat fried chicken!" she chuckled, pushing him toward the door.

ALONE, LUCY PEELED off her stockings and, with a single movement of her hands, drew off her knitted blouse and skirt. The accuracy of Tom's earlier remark was verified. There wasn't a bit of lingerie underneath her outer costume!

Creamy skin, softly fleshed contours, the richness of silky brown curls and brown eyes, gorgeously cherry-tipped breasts, a kiss-expectant mouth . . . all of her charms blended into a composite of loveliness that was pulsing with the passionate yearning of ripe maturity.

She threw herself down on the bed and struck a match for a cigarette which she extracted from the package that Tom had left her.

"Bathing in a bucket!" she smiled. "That's supposed to be a lot of fun! . . . Well, maybe it would be, if somebody nice was bathing you, but I prefer a bathtub or a shower."

She ran her hands over her hips and waist and breasts.

"I've never been so hot in my life as I was today!" she thought. "And now I've got to bathe in a bucket!"

She thrust out a lissom leg and dipped a toe in the water. "Nice and cool!" she murmured, gliding off the bed.

A small window, draped with a white linen curtain, attracted her attention. She parted the curtain and gazed out. Through the trees, the lake basked in the last rays of the setting sun.

"I haven't had a swim in ages!" she said. "If I only brought along a swimming suit!"

The cigarette bobbed from her crimson mouth. "But it *would* be fun to swim without a suit . . . to let the water lap around me all over . . . cool and sweet . . . it would be the first thrill I've had on this crazy trip that Tom suggested."

There was a wooded hillock within range of her vision, and the lake stretched beyond.

"Nobody could see me if I strolled down there and slid into the water!"

She looked disdainfully at the bucket of water. "Tom can use that, if he wants to be a camper. . . . I'm going to take a swim!"

Hurriedly, she slipped into her knitted dress. Through the door of the cabin she sauntered, walking nonchalantly in the direction of the lake and humming a song. "I love to feel the water in my bathtub flexing about my bare breasts!" she thought. "I've never felt a lake caressing me all over."

She crossed the hillock and glanced backward. The countryside was bare of human occupancy. It was as if she was on a desert island, alone with her beauty and the enticing water.

Under an overhanging tree, she took off her shoes and slid her dress downward. The evening breeze caressed her bare skin, and its comforting zephyrs made her gasp. "There's something to this auto touring, after all!" she sighed, sinking her fingers into the voluptuous extravagance of twin mounds. . . . She walked toward the water. . . . Her bare feet touched its cool edge. . . . Onward she moved. . . . The water crept upward, along her legs, past her knees, inch by inch along her thighs. . . . It enveloped her hips, lapped about her waist, and finally reached the rounded eminences of her breasts.

"Heavenly!" whispered Lucy.

Slowly she sank into the water, and struck out with graceful strokes, swimming a dozen yards, floating peacefully, swimming again, exhilarated by the wavelets aroused by her thrashing arms.

But the hunger of a healthy tummy called her shoreward. "Fried chicken!" she thought.

She was on the point of arising from the water when her eyes caught a glimpse of something that made her pause. . . . A young man was sitting on the embankment of the lake, evidently enjoying the view! . . . And he was not more than three feet away from the spot where her dress lay!

Lucy paddled around, flustered with embarrassment.

"Hello!" said the young man. "You don't mind a gentleman here?"

"If you were a gentleman you wouldn't be sitting there!" she stated, emphatically.

"Gentlemen are partial to beauty!" he retorted. "And if I know what constitutes beauty, then I am indeed a lucky individual!"

"Go away!" said Lucy. "You're a fresh boy!"

"No, you're wrong!" he grinned. "I'm not

fresh, but appreciative of all the good things in life."

"Go away!" she stated, again. "I'd like to come out of this lake. . . . It was swell at first, but it's getting very cold now . . . and fried chicken awaits me with my husband!"

"Fried chicken!" he echoed. "That's something, isn't it?"

"Oh, beat it!" said Lucy, becoming exasperated. . . . The heat of the day had evaaporated, and the chill of the lake water was giving her the creepy effect of goose pimples now. "I don't feel like carrying on a conversation at this minute . . . this water's getting very cold!"

"If you only knew how beautiful you look, swimming around like one of the mermaids you read about!" He heaved a sigh. "Girly, girly, girly! Where have *you* been all my life?"

"None of your business!" retorted Lucy. "Will you please go away . . . or, at least, turn your back so I can get my dress?"

"The latter request is reasonable!" he said. "Here is your dress . . . tell me when you're presentable!" He swung around, his back to her.

Lucy came out of the lake and swiftly grabbed her dress. . . . Over her damp brown curls it went!

"You're so young that you think you're irresistible!" she murmured, smoothing the knit silk over her hips. "If my husband were here, he would change the geography of your face for you."

"Husbands!" said he. "Inconvenient males they are . . . husbands!"

Lucy shivered. . . . She had stayed in the water a little too long. . . . The sun might have been hot in the daytime, but the lake at evening was cold indeed!

"Have a cigarette?" he asked.

Lucy ordinarily would have darted a glance of derision at him and walked away. . . . But her heart was pounding excitedly. . . . Here on the banks of a lake on the Shenandoah countryside an uncommonly good looking young man had seen all of her that was to be seen, and he seemed to be much impressed by what he saw. . . . She took the cigarette and lighted it from the same match that ignited his own.

"There wasn't anybody here when I went in swimming!" she said. "I am wondering where in the world you came from?"

"Does it matter?" he replied. "Sit down on the grass and let's get thoroughly acquainted."

The thrill that went through Lucy was acute! . . . In this lonely spot she had encountered a young man whose personality was more attractive than any other she had met, notwithstanding the country clubs and the dancing and the social entertainments of the city.

A farmer lad, she thought, even though his conversation was not. . . . A college boy, probably, working the summer through on a hillside farm, and sitting by the lake in the cool of the evening. . . . She would never see him again!

Lucy sat down on the grass. "Who are you?"

"Who cares?" he whispered. "Who are you?"

"Who knows?" she murmured.

His arm encircled her, reveling in the softness of her waist and the warmth of her protruding breasts. . . . Lucy didn't protest. . . . The shadows of the evening were lengthening, her passionate soul responded to the sweet romance of the occasion. . . . Her face lifted to meet his kiss!

"Oh, heavens alive!" she gasped, a minute later. "You're surely not a farm boy, are you?"

"Does it matter?" he said, sliding the knitted dress from her smooth shoulder and pressing his lips to the sweet hollow of her arm. "We met, we saw, we kissed!"

"Was it fate?" Lucy breathed.

"It was a dream that came true!" he muttered.

"What brought you down to the lake this evening?" she asked.

"This is where I wait for my dream girl every evening." He captured her mouth and drew her back on the grass.

Lucy gasped. "Oh! . . . Oh! . . . Oh!"

The sun dipped below the horizon. . . . The lake gently caressed the shore, and all was peaceful except the amorous merger of two souls!

"DELICIOUS CHICKEN, isn't it?" said Tom, somewhat later.

"Marvelous!" agreed Lucy.

Tom heartily gazed at her. "If you don't like this auto tour, we'll turn back and spend the rest of our vacation somewhere else!"

"We won't!" said Lucy. "There is romance in an auto tour, after all, darling."

"What made you change your mind?"

"Don't ask questions!" she whispered. "Join me in another piece of this chicken . . . the breast is delicious!"

A PILLOW OF GREEN

By R. L. TRUMAN

(*Conclusion*)

AS THEY DROVE, Vic discovered, as many others had, that the warm evenings of *Los Claros Cielos* bring exhilarating, equally warm, winds that make leisurely driving under a huge bronze moon, through tall, somberly dark redwoods, an excellent reason for slipping an arm about the fragrant, perfumed softness of curves deliciously feminine.

"Still feel like apologizing?" Chloe presently asked, throwing her head back against the rolled top and breathing deeply, a motion that brought her round, full breasts into play and drew her tight-fitting skirt up and up until several bare inches of lovely white thigh became distractingly visible. Moonlight played upon her tantalizing voluptuous charms and bathed them in a golden color that was, like Chloe, ripe and warm—irresistibly desirable!

Vic stopped the car beneath a grove of trees and drew her to his side. Imagine his amazement when, after a brief, thoroughly tame kiss, she pushed him away.

"Is your suit in the car?" she asked, to Vic's bewilderment.

"No-o—" he answered, then he remembered that he did have a pair of swimming trunks stowed away somewhere in the back.

"That's too bad," Chloe muttered, "for I've always wanted to drive through the moonlight—this way—"

With actions to fit her words, she tugged at her frock and was soon holding it, neatly folded, in one tiny hand! And—there was Chloe, her lush contours threatening to burst the diaphanous, clinging silk brassiere and panties that the beach "copper" had found outrageous! In less than ten seconds, or so it seemed to Chloe, Vic had donned his trunks!

They drove on for several minutes and then she pointed through the trees, extending a firm, slender arm that he promptly kissed.

"There's a beach down there," she said, squirming playfully as his lips slid along her arm, finally resting upon a warm, deliriously thrilling, firm peak of snowy-white flesh. "And, besides, I want to explain something to you—"

"Darling," Vic whispered, "if you say swim, I'll even *swim* tonight!"

"That's just what I *was* going to say, you dear!" she laughed, leading the way out of the car.

Chloe was the first in, but Vic quickly followed her. The water was delightfully warm and, side by side, they swam upstream. Overhead, the sky was a star-studded bowl of dark blue.

" Ooooooh!" Chloe suddenly cried. "I—I think—my leg—it's cramped! Vic! Vic!"

Swimming to her, he supported her, placing his arm over her ripe little breasts, and, even in this predicament, he could not help enjoying the sensation caused by having such soft, round twin beauties pressed thrillingly against his arm.

"Are you all right, sweet?" he asked, his senses burning as hard little tips of crimson flesh crushed against his bare arm.

"I—I think so—" Chloe answered weakly, struggling to keep her head above water. "But—sweetheart — my leg—it hurts so! Don't—don't let me go—it's so terribly dark!"

"Hardly!" Vic panted, tightening his hold upon her sweet little hillocks. "Hardly!"

Once safely on the beach, he briskly massaged her numbed thighs, not an altogether unpleasant task. . . . Then he hurried back to the car and returned with a large, wooly robe.

"O.K. now?" he asked, wrapping her in it. "How about a little drink?"

He disappeared again and soon Chloe was gratefully sampling the contents of his flask.

"You have some, too—" she whispered and Vic obliged. "But—I—I don't need this robe —it's so warm—"

She flung it aside, relaxed her perfectly proportioned contours on the sand, and Vic found his pulse throbbing to the exciting picture of lovely Chloe in silken, wet and clinging panties—and flimsy bandeaux!

"You—you don't have to apologize now, dear," she murmured, "but you should know two things—"

"What are they?" Vic asked, resting at her side.

"First, I hit you with that ball—on purpose—"

"Forgiven!" Vic interrupted. "Proceed—"

"Then, later, I let you look for me, when you thought I had drowned, and—"

"And what?" asked Vic, his lips slowly drawing closer to a distracting little dimple that nestled on her smooth, milky-white shoulders.

"Well, I watched you all the time and thought you were a scream—but I don't think it's funny tonight—"

Vic hardly heard her words, seeing only the inviting, soft warmness of her quivering lips. Passionately, he kissed her, firmly, possessively, as his hands feverishly caressed the tempting flesh of each delicious, pearly-white mound. More eagerly than ever he explored the thrilling, rounded charms that Chloe had in such abundance. . . .

Only a brassiere, calmly floating down the river *La Almohada de la Verde* knew that Chloe discarded it herself, and only a silken scanty knew that she had experienced nary a cramp. . . .

(Continued from page 2)

your letters. I promise to answer them all.

And many thanks to you, Mr. Editor.

Sincerely, E. James Allard, Jr.

Salem Street, Reading, Mass.

Dear Editor:

I should like to correspond with some of "Spicy Stories" readers.

I am 22 years old, brunette, blue eyes, attractive, musician, love books and write stories. Love sports.

I like to write letters and write interesting ones.

We can meet if any of the writers come to Chicago to see the World's Fair. La Grange is a suberb of Chicago.

Sincerely, (Miss) Bonnie Jordan.

General Delivery, La Grange, Ill.

(*Continued from page* 51)

A motor launch was cruising about, and standing at the edge of the water, Judy hailed it. It came towards her and ran in close to the shore. Stew was at the helm. Lifting her dress to her waist, Judy waded out to the boat and clambered aboard. Before Stew could say anything, she said, "I'll tell you all about it, later, Stew. Still want to marry me?" Stew nodded eagerly. "All right." Judy went forward, and sat down on a thwart. Stew was about to head the launch upstream when there came a loud hail from the bush. Ronnie, in just trousers, came bounding down the beach. He waded to the boat and joined Judy on the thwart. Breathlessly, he said,

"What's the idea of leaving me, lady?"

Judy made up her mind, tears came into her eyes and she told him everything. Ronnie listened intently, and when she had finished, he was grinning. All he said was, "Do you love me?"

"Yes," answered Judy weakly. "That's why I couldn't go through with it."

Ronnie took her shivering little body in his arms and held her close. "Home, James," he said to Stew. "How'd you like to be best man at my wedding?"

"Lousy," said the unhappy Stew. Judy was smiling, and she deliberately placed Ronnie's hand around her waist.

(*Continued from page* 28)

pered, sitting beside him. "A kiss in the dawn . . . nice, isn't it?"

"You're tired, darling boy! Relax, just relax!" she cautioned.

(*To be continued*)

(*Continued from page* 14)

Terence held his breath. "Yes . . . yes . . ."

"—told me that O'Toole was a—was a—"

"Yes . . . yes!"

"—a sucker for a dame. So I—"

In one motion, Terence was pulling on his blue jumper. He wanted to say things but the words stuck in his throat. Toddy sat up, astonished.

"Jackie!" she cried. "What's the matter?"

No answer.

"Jackie! What are you doing?" Her breasts were white and full in the lamp light, but Terence was oblivious to their charm.

"Jackie! Jackie! JACKIE!"

The door slammed shut behind Mr. O'Toole.

THE BROAD WATERS of the lower Hudson, black from the oil drippings of snub-nosed tugs and heavy with the stench of melted tar from the ferryboat docks, caught the strident moans of a hundred steam whistles from every manner of dingy river craft and hurled them back at the smoky sky with three-fold resonance.

Like a giant grey caterpillar, the Atlantic Fleet moved down river, pointing towards the Narrows and the open sea.

It was all the old stuff to Terence Rafferty O'Toole, and his red, pug-nosed face showed it as he leaned against the forward rail of the *U. S. S. Brevoort* and watched the jagged edge of the New York skyline fade away.

It was old stuff, and yet, something new had happened to take the edge off the monotony. A much handled letter, addressed to Jack Riley, which Terence had claimed, was clutched in his hand. He read it for the tenth time.

Darling Jack:

I don't know why you left so suddenly and I don't care. I will wait for you because I'm all through following the fleet.

Love,

Toddy.

Terence grinned. Well, they hadn't waited for Terence O'Toole! Maybe they'd wait for Jack Riley? He hummed a little tune as the guns of Fort Hamilton boomed . . . for him!

(*Continued on page* 8)

"Just a moment and I'll get it." Returning, she handed the note to Hyde. He opened it and read. She saw his face go gray as he perused the lines that Sandra had written.

"Gone back to start on my next picture. Follow me out here and I'll have you arrested on a charge of annoying me the moment I lay eyes on you.

". . . Thanks for a lot of lessons. I don't think we owe each other anything; you had your fun, and you saved my job for me. They refused to take up my option unless I cut my weight twenty-five pounds; which, thanks to you, I did.

Sandra."

Blank Cartridge Pistol

REVOLVER STYLE

.22 CAL. **MADE IN 3 SIZES** **25c 50c $1.00**

Three new models now out 25c, 50c and $1.00. Well made and effective. Modelled on pattern of latest type of Revolver. Appearance alone enough to scare a burglar. Takes 22 Cal. Blank Cartridges obtainable everywhere. Great protection against burglars, tramps, dogs. Have it lying around without the danger attached to other revolvers. Fine for 4th July, New Years, for stage work, starting pistol, etc. **SMALL SIZE 4 in. long 25c. MEDIUM SIZE 5 in. long 50c. LARGE SIZE 6in. long $1.00. BLANK CARTRIDGES 50c per 100. HOLSTER (Cowboy type) 50c. Shipped by Express only not prepaid.** *Big catalog of other pistols, sporting goods, etc. 10 cents.*

BOYS! THROW YOUR VOICE

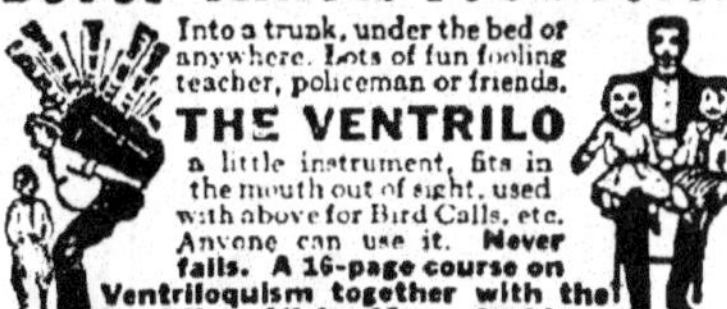

Into a trunk, under the bed or anywhere. Lots of fun fooling teacher, policeman or friends.

THE VENTRILO

a little instrument, fits in the mouth out of sight, used with above for Bird Calls, etc. Anyone can use it. **Never fails. A 16-page course on Ventriloquism together with the Ventrilo. All for 10c postpaid.**

CHAMELEONS

25 Cents Each. Shipped By Mail

LIVE, SAFE DELIVERY GUARANTEED

Watch it change its color!

Get one of these most wonderful of all creatures. Watch it change its color. Study its habits. Wear one on the lapel of your coat as a curiosity. Watch it shoot out its tongue as it catches flies and insects for food. No trouble to keep. Can go for months without food. Measures about 5 inches in length. Shipped to any address in U. S. A. by mail. We guarantee safe arrival and live delivery. **PRICE 25 CENTS, OR 3 FOR 50 CENTS POSTPAID.**

Novelty French Photo Ring

Here is a very great novelty in Rings, that is selling in thousands. It is a nicely made ring, finished in imitation platinum, and set with a large imitation diamond. It looks just like an ordinary ring, but in the shank of the ring is a small microscopic picture almost invisible to the naked eye, yet is magnified to an almost incredible degree and with astonishing clearness. There is quite an assortment of pictures that should suit all tastes. Some are pictures of bathing girl beauties, pretty French Actresses, etc., others are views of places of interest in France, Panama Canal and elsewhere; others show the Lord's Prayer in type, every word of which can be read by persons with normal eyesight. They are interesting without being in any way objectionable. **PRICE 25c. 3 for 65c. or $2.25 per doz. postpaid.** *BIG CATALOG* 10c

REAL LIVE PET TURTLES 25c

If you want a fascinating and interesting little pet, just risk 25c and we will send you a real live **PET TURTLE** by mail postpaid. Thousands sold at Chicago Worlds Fair. No trouble at all to keep. Just give it a little lettuce or cabbage or let it seek its own food. Extremely gentle, easily kept and live for years and years. Need less attention than any other pet. Get one or more. Study their habits. You will find them extremely interesting. **Price 25c.** SPECIAL TURTLE FOOD **10c pkg.**

THE FAN DANCE

PRICE 10 CENTS

HOTSY TOTSY

HIT *of the* CENTURY *of* PROGRESS

Who will forget the famous FAN DANCE episode of the Century of Progress Exposition in Chicago? Here it is humorously, cleanly presented in vest pocket form. You flip the pages and **HOTSY TOTSY** comes to life and whirls through her dance, provoking not a sly smile, but a wholesome laugh from all, even the most fastidious. It is a most innocent fun maker that will cause you and your friends no end of fun and amusement. **HOTSY TOTSY the FAN DANCER** measures only 2 x 3 inches – 6 square inches of spicy, piquant entertainment for one and all. **PRICE 10c.** Add 3c for postage. *Big Catalog* **10c.**

Johnson Smith & Co., Dep. 602 Racine, Wis.

MAKE YOUR OWN RADIO RECEIVING SET

Enjoy the concerts, baseball games, market reports, latest news, etc. This copyrighted book "EFFICIENT RADIO SETS" shows how to make and operate inexpensive Radio Sets, the materials for which can be purchased for a mere trifle. Also tells how to build a short-wave Receiver for bringing in foreign stations, police calls, ships at sea, etc. **ONLY 15c. postpaid.**

SILENT DEFENDER

Used by police officers, detectives, sheriffs, night watchmen and others as a means of self-protection. Very effective. Easily fits the hand, the fingers being grasped in the four holes. Very useful in an emergency. Made of aluminum they are very light, weighing less than 2 ounces. Handy pocket size always ready for instant use. **PRICE 25c each, 2 for 45c postpaid.**

HOW TO WIN AT POKER

Written by a card sharper. Tells how to win at draw poker. Explains different varieties of poker such as Straight Poker, Stud Poker, Whiskey Poker, Mistigris, The Freeze-out, The Widow, Rice, Jack Pots, etc. Exposes the methods used by card sharpers and professional gamblers. 13 Chapters. This book contains a vast amount of information and may save you from being fleeced by crooked players and gamblers. **PRICE 10c Postpaid.** *Big Novelty Catalog 10 Cents*

MAGIC MADE EASY 250 MAGIC TRICKS

An excellent little book containing 250 Parlor tricks, tricks with cards, coins, handkerchiefs, eggs, rings, glasses, etc. So simple that a child can perform them. Profusely illus. **Price Postpaid 10c; 3 copies 25c.**

125 CARD TRICKS and sleight of hand. Contains all the latest and best card tricks as performed by celebrated magicians, with exposé of card tricks used by professional gamblers. **PRICE 25c POSTPAID.**

Wonderful X-Ray Tube

A wonderful little instrument producing optical illusions both surprising and startling. With it you can see what is apparently the bones of your fingers, the lead in a lead pencil, the interior opening in a pipe stem, and many other similar illusions. **Price 10c, 3 for 25c.**

Fortune Telling By Cards

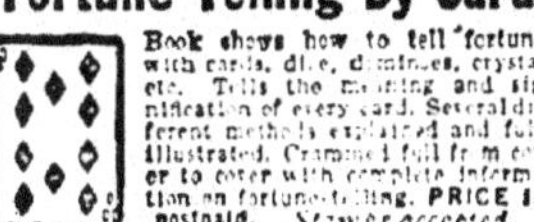

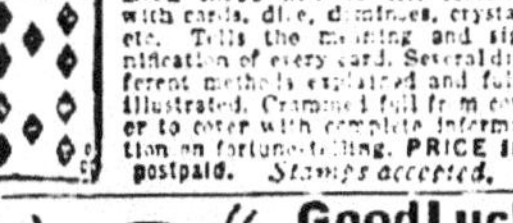

Book shows how to tell fortunes with cards, dice, dominoes, crystal, etc. Tells the meaning and signification of every card. Several different methods explained and fully illustrated. Crammed full from cover to cover with complete information on fortune-telling. **PRICE 10c postpaid.** *Stamps accepted.*

Good Luck RING

Very striking, quaint and uncommon. Oxidized gunmetal finish, with two brilliant flashing imitation rubies or emeralds sparkling out of the eyes. Said to bring good luck to the wearer. **PRICE 25c Postpaid**

HOW TO PITCH Pitch the Fade-away, Spitter, Knuckler, Smoke Ball, etc. Lessons by leading Big League Pitchers. Clearly illustrated and described with 78 pictures. **POSTPAID 25c**

Electric Telegraph Set 15c

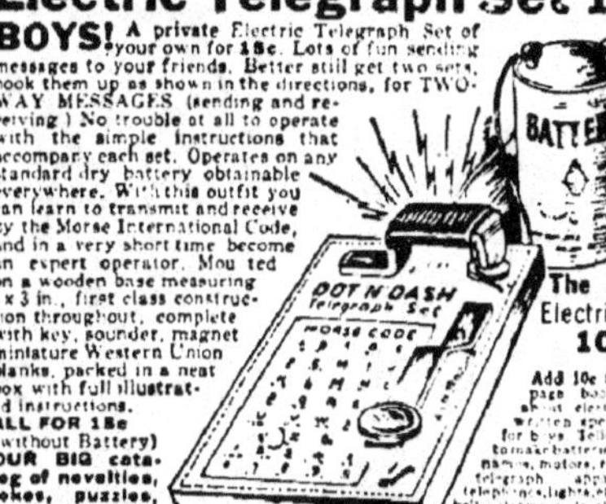

BOYS! A private Electric Telegraph Set of your own for **15c.** Lots of fun sending messages to your friends. Better still get two sets, hook them up as shown in the directions, for TWO-WAY MESSAGES (sending and receiving.) No trouble at all to operate with the simple instructions that accompany each set. Operates on any standard dry battery obtainable everywhere. With this outfit you can learn to transmit and receive by the Morse International Code, and in a very short time become an expert operator. Mounted on a wooden base measuring 4 x 3 in., first class construction throughout, complete with key, sounder, magnet miniature Western Union blanks, packed in a neat box with full illustrated instructions. **ALL FOR 15c** (without Battery) **OUR BIG catalog of novelties, jokes, puzzles, tricks, etc. 10c**

The Boy Electrician 10c Add 10c for 84 page book all about electricity written specially for boys. Tells how to make batteries, dynamos, motors, radios, telegraph apparatus, telephones, lights, electric bells, alarms, coils, electric engines. **PRICE 10c ppd.**

LIVE BABY ALLIGATOR $1.00

How would you like a *Safe Delivery Guaranteed* real live Baby Alligator for your very own? A craze for Baby Alligator pets has swept the country. We have arranged, at great expense, to supply you with a **GENUINE LIVE BABY ALLIGATOR.** Just hatched in the deep marshlands of the South, at an amazingly low price. These darling little pets will be shipped to you by mail, carefully packed—safe arrival guaranteed. Think of the fun, the thrills you will have with one of these Baby Alligators. Read how fascinating they are, how interesting. Study nature. Remember, the alligator comes down to us from prehistoric days, from the age of dinosaurs! Do you want a Baby Alligator? You bet you do. What boy wouldn't? **PRICE $1.00 postpaid.**

HORNED TOADS 25c EACH

LIVE DELIVERY GUARANTEED

Horned Toads—most interesting pets. Head, back and sides armed with long, horny spikes. Although of apparently sluggish nature, when in search of food it runs like lightning. Watch it pounce upon flies. Amusement by the hour. No trouble at all to keep. Feed it on meal worms or let it seek its own food. Will live for years and years. Shipped by mail to any address in U. S. A. or Canada for **25 cents**

BIG ENTERTAINER 15c

326 Jokes and Riddles, 25 Magic Tricks, 10 Parlor Games, 73 Toasts, 13 Fairy Tales, 105 Money-making Secrets, 22 Monologues, 21 Puzzles and Problems, 5 Comic Recitations, 10 Funny Readings, 11 Parlor Pastimes, 13 Flirtations, 1110 Girls' and Boys' Names and their Meanings, 10 Picture Puzzles, 60 Amusing Rhymes, 37 Amusing Experiments, Deaf and Dumb Alphabet, Shadowgraphy, Gypsy Fortune Teller, How to tell Fortunes with Cards, Dice, Dominoes, Crystal, Coffee Cup, etc. Hypnotism, Ventriloquism, Cut-outs for Checkers and Chess, Dominoes, Fox and Geese, 9 Men Morris, Spanish Prison Puzzle, Game of Anagrams, 25 Card Tricks, Crystal Gazing, etc. **ALL FOR 15c.** *Novelty Catalog 10c*

TELL YOUR OWN FORTUNE

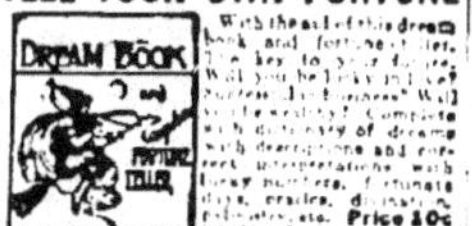

With the aid of this dream book and fortune-teller. The key to your future. Will you be lucky in life? Success in business? Will your love be true? Complete with dictionary of dreams with descriptions and correct interpretations with lucky numbers, fortunate days, oracles, divination, palmistry, etc. **Price 10c postpaid.**

Learn to Hypnotize

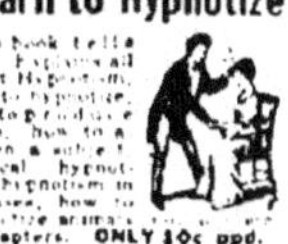

This book tells how. Explains all about Hypnotism, how to hypnotize, how to produce sleep, how to awaken a subject. Medical hypnotism, hypnotism in diseases, how to hypnotize animals [illegible] 25 chapters. **ONLY 10c ppd.**

HOME BREWED WINES BEERS

This book contains over 100 simple recipes, with full instructions, for making all kinds of wines, beers, cider, elder champagne, brandies, gin, rum, whiskey, fruit cordials and simple liqueurs, fruit syrups, various kinds of vinegars, etc., etc. Home made wines and beers are particularly good and wholesome and their manufacture is not difficult. **PRICE 10c ppd.**

Merry Widow Handkerchief

A perfect model of the most necessary lingerie garment worn by the ladies which, when folded up and worn in the pocket, has the appearance of being a gentleman's handkerchief. A very clever and mirthful joker. **PRICE 15c ppd.**

JOHNSON SMITH & CO., DEPT. 602, RACINE, WIS.

ADDRESS ORDERS FOR GOODS ON THIS PAGE TO

JOHNSON SMITH & CO.

DEPT. 602 **RACINE, WISCONSIN**

Our complete Catalog sent on receipt of 10c, or the De Luxe Cloth Bound Edition for 25c. Bigger and better than ever. Only book of its kind in existence. Describes thousands of all the latest tricks in magic, the newest novelties, puzzles, games, sporting goods, rubber stamps, unusual and interesting books, curiosities in seeds and plants, etc., many unprocurable elsewhere. Remit by Coin, Money Order or Postage Stamps.

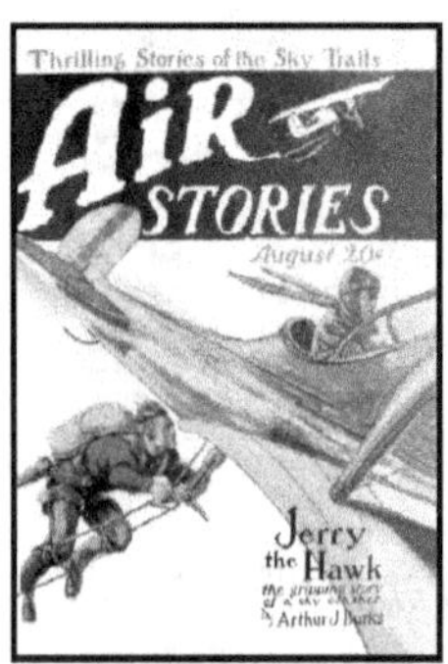

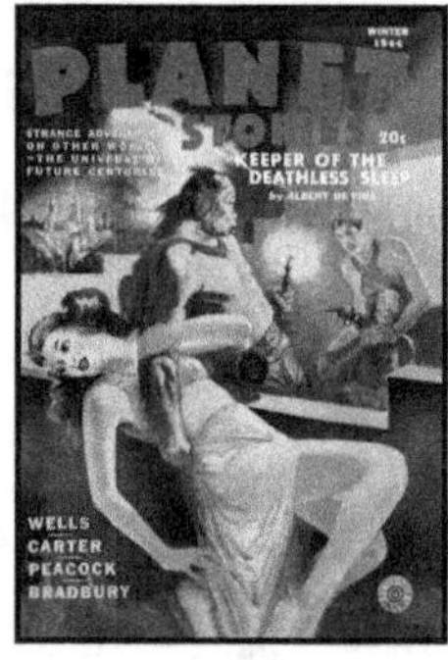

The Fiction House Press Replica Line is available at
www.FictionHousePress.com

Be sure to check our website regularly as we are constantly adding more
pulp and digest replicas to our lineup.

www.ingramcontent.com/pod-product-compliance
Lightning Source LLC
LaVergne TN
LVHW061254100826
845148LV00008B/1125